In a curious way, those days are pleasant to think back on. They were satisfying. I kept busy doing all my favorite things, so I never got lonely. August found me lying on the grass, or floating on the lake, or skimming the boat across the glassy blue water. I felt warm and healed up. The lake always did that to me.

But then there were the nights. That was when my father's death came to me, trying to work its way in like a pet I'd left out in the cold. *What about me,* it said. And then the dreams started. Dark images, shadows on the wall, presences that felt real. I'd wake up, sweating, sometimes crying. I'd have to stare at the lake until I felt safe again. Its waters sloshing back and forth sounded familiar and comforting. The lake had always been there; it would always be there. It wouldn't abandon me. When the shoreline was edged in pink I'd fall asleep again, full of hope.

That was how my life was unfolding that August—that strange summer when my father died, when I met Abby, when everything got as bizarre as it could get, then got worse.

The
House
Across
the Cove

The House Across the Cove

BARBARA HALL

LAUREL-LEAF BOOKS

Published by
Bantam Doubleday Dell Books for Young Readers
a division of
Bantam Doubleday Dell Publishing Group, Inc.
1540 Broadway
New York, New York 10036

ISBN: 0-440-21938-8

RL: 5.1

Book design by Claire Vaccaro

Cover photo illustration by Kathleen Creighton

Printed in the United States of America

September 1995

10 9 8 7 6 5 4 3 2 1

To my parents for enduring my adventures, and to Molly Noah for believing in them.

TYLER

Chapter 1

That summer was strange from the very beginning. June was cold and misty. July it rained most of the month, one thunderstorm after another. Trees fell, creeks overflowed, Flanders Lake rose above the shoreline, up to the doors of the cabins and trailers. Boats sank or were ravaged against the docks. Some of the docks themselves got washed away and went sailing down the lake like battered vessels.

It seemed like the only house on Bolwood Cove that didn't suffer any damage was the one right across the water, the one I saw every time I looked out the window of the trailer. It was supposed to have cost at least a million dollars to build, and no one had ever lived there. It belonged, so they said, to a Dr. Kaplan from Norwood, who named it Lucinda after his wife. We just called it The House.

I watched it endure the summer storms, the lashing rains and merciless winds. But I never saw a board break, a gutter sag, or a window crack. It just kept standing, strong and proud, as if it might be sneering at the weaker houses, laughing at them.

August it turned warm and sticky, so humid you could feel the air on your skin, like a hot damp cloth. The sun was out almost every day. The mosquitoes buzzed, the frogs croaked, the lake retreated. The land dried up and chigger weeds sprouted. Crickets hid in them, talking at sunset. It was the way summer was supposed to be. Almost.

I was sixteen, and it was the first summer I'd lived away from home. I'd been in love with Flanders Lake ever since I could remember, and always dreamed of living there one day. But by the time I got my chance, I was ready to forget that dream.

The trailer in question didn't belong to me or my family. It belonged to my best friend, Rodney Stone. His folks had bought it when we were ten and they used to go there all the time and take us. Then they lost interest and stopped going, but Rod and I never got bored with it. We went up every chance we got. His folks didn't care. They let us stay, they let us use the boat, they even gave us money for groceries. I couldn't ever decide if they were being generous or just trying to get us out of the way. But then, I've never been great at understanding parents.

When my father died that summer, the first day of June, I needed a place to live. My mother completely freaked out. Of course, her connection to reality had never been all that strong. You know how every family has a crazy Aunt Somebody? Well, that was my mother. Crazy Aunt Jo. Not flighty, eccentric, wacky, scatterbrained, laugh-a-minute type crazy. Honest-to-goodness, shock-treatment and antidepressants type crazy.

I'm aware that I'm not supposed to use the word crazy. I'm supposed to use specific medical phraseology, like manic-depressive or general personality disorder. But since my mother has never been diagnosed by a doctor, it's hard to talk about the nature of her problem. She's just not in the same orbit as the rest of us.

So when Dad died, Mom's sisters swooped down on her like pigeons on bread crumbs and whisked her away. They knew if they left her alone she'd be in an institution in no time. My aunts volunteered to take me in, too. But when I said no, I had other plans, they didn't look too disappointed.

Rodney's parents were going on some extended trip around the country in a Winnebago. They'd always thought of me as family, so they told me I could stay in the trailer for the summer. Rod went with them for part of the trip, but then he came back. He came to the lake every other weekend to hang out with me, and the rest of the time he stayed in town so he could work. I had a part-time job building and repairing docks at the lake. It was pretty steady after July. Everybody and his brother needed a new one.

In a curious way, those days are pleasant to think back on. They were satisfying. I kept busy doing all my favorite things, so I never got lonely. August found me lying on the grass, or floating on the lake, or skimming the boat across the glassy blue water. I felt warm and healed up. The lake always did that to me.

But then there were the nights. That was when my father's death came to me, trying to work its way in like a pet I'd left out in the cold. *What about me,* it said. And then the dreams started. Dark images, shadows on the wall, presences that felt real. I'd wake up, sweating, sometimes crying. I'd have to stare at the lake until I felt safe again. Its waters sloshing back and forth sounded familiar and comforting. The lake had always been there; it would always be there. It wouldn't abandon me. When the shoreline was edged in pink I'd fall asleep again, full of hope.

That was how my life was unfolding that August—that strange summer when my father died, when I met Abby, when everything got as bizarre as it could get, then got worse.

Chapter 2

It was a Monday when I got a call to go fix the dock at the Wheats' cabin. Tom Wheat was a good guy, kind of eccentric, moving into his late fifties and trying to write a novel. He came to the lake to escape his regular life. He needed the solitude to finish up his by now colossal manuscript, something he'd been working on for years. But whenever he found himself completely alone, he started looking for distractions. As I headed over there with my toolbox, I had a feeling his dock didn't need that much mending.

"I don't like this board here," Tom said, bouncing up and down on it. "Sounds like it's trying to break away."

He was wearing a ratty old sweatshirt and jeans, battered tennis shoes, and tortoiseshell glasses. If you saw Tom on the street you'd say to yourself, "struggling writer."

I examined the board, which was a little

weatherworn, but stable. It would hold at least a summer, maybe more.

"I could replace it," I said, "but I'd have to tear up a couple of other boards in the process and it'd cost you a mint."

He nodded, chewing on an unlit pipe he'd pulled out of his pocket.

"Is it worth it?" he asked.

"I don't think so. It's pretty sturdy."

"Well, Tyler," he said, slapping me on the shoulder, "I trust your judgment on this matter. You haven't steered me wrong yet."

"No, sir."

He hesitated, staring at me as he continued to chew his pipe. I could tell he wanted conversation.

"How's everything else?" I asked.

"What else? There is no 'else' to a writer's life. There's the pursuit of the written word, and when that stops, you're left with a boring old man with bad teeth."

"I don't think you're boring."

"God bless you, Tyler Crane. You hungry?"

"No, sir."

"Cut this 'sir' crap. I'm not a knight. I can't even finish my book."

"How's that going?"

"I'd rather talk about drinking. You thirsty?"

I said I was, though I'd finished half a quart of orange juice before I came over. I knew he needed the company so I followed him inside.

His cabin was a small but well-built A-frame. Some of the cabins on the lake were really well designed and might have been in some architectural magazine if they hadn't been hidden away on a lake in the middle of No-where, Virginia.

Flanders was a mill town, full of families with old money. Flanders Lake was a resort about fifteen miles from the town itself. It was built during the fifties, as a place for families to get away from the dreary smells and sounds of the mills that had made them rich. At least that was my way of looking at it.

I wasn't from one of those old-money fami-lies, but that didn't make me love the lake any less. Nor did the fact that it wasn't a natural wonder; it was man-made. Five hundred miles of shoreline carved out of the wilderness. Flan-ders Dam was one of the biggest of its kind on the East Coast, and the area soon became the closest thing western Virginia had to a tourist attraction. None of that mattered to me. All I knew was that every time I stepped outside the trailer, I saw miles and miles of startling blue water, and great cedars and pines and oaks and maples rising up to greet the clouds.

"What's your poison?" Tom asked me as he poured himself a tumblerful of white wine.

"Something soft. Soda or juice."

"You're a wise man. This stuff will kill you," he said, but didn't sound like he believed it.

We sat at his kitchen table, which was right in front of a large plate glass window. The sun blazed rebelliously over the lake, as if to say, "I'm back, and you better believe it." We sat and watched skiers and sailboats and speeders whipping across the water.

Tom asked, "How's your family?"

I looked at the pulp floating in my juice and said, "Well, unfortunately my father passed away."

Tom looked truly stricken. "I'm sorry, kid."

I shrugged.

"You holding up all right?" he asked.

"I guess so."

"Well, you know where I am, day or night. Drop by anytime. I can use the company."

"I wouldn't want to interrupt your writing."

"You wouldn't interrupt anything but pacing at the moment. I've hit a block the size of the

Berlin Wall. Or what used to be the Berlin Wall. I can't even keep up with the world. You ever feel like that, Tyler?"

"All the time," I said.

We were interrupted by a knock at the door. Tom seemed annoyed but assumed a cheerful expression as he went to answer it.

"Clark, how the hell are you?" I heard Tom say. He was starting to sound a little drunk.

There was some mumbling at the door, and then Tom said, "Sure, he's here. Come on in."

I stood up as a tall, distinguished-looking man entered the room. He was wearing a white cotton sweater, Polo jeans, and navy boat shoes. His skin was tanned. He looked to be a little younger than Tom, and much more composed. This man was rich.

"Tyler, do you know my neighbor, Clark Ramsey?"

We shook hands as I tried to think of an appropriate reply. I knew who he was all right, even though I'd never met him face-to-face. He was one of the wealthiest men in the county. He owned a couple of mills and had a winery on the side. He also had a daughter named Alexandria who was in my class at school. She was only in my class in the academic sense. Otherwise, Zan Ramsey and I were worlds apart.

Zan was a stunner. She was the kind of girl who made you slump when you saw her—because she was so perfect and because your chances were so remote. She made me feel invisible. I was just the son of an unstable housewife and an insurance salesman.

Stumped for an answer, I finally came up with what seemed to be the worst possible choice.

"I know your daughter," I said.

I felt his grip loosen around my hand.

"Oh?"

"Well, we're both sophomores at Flanders High. Or juniors now, I guess."

He nodded, studying me hard. His eyes were gray blue. His nose was perfect in shape and angle, like Zan's.

"Your name again?" he asked.

"Tyler Crane."

His nod suggested that it meant nothing to him either way.

"I saw you out there looking at Tom's dock. Is that your line of work or were you just doing Tom a favor?"

"A little of both," Tom answered for me. "He's the best dock repairman around, and he does me a favor every time he drops by. Great conversationalist. Well, to be honest, a great listener. No one can get a word in around me."

Tom poured himself another healthy dose of wine and waved the bottle at Mr. Ramsey, who shook his head.

"Are you available this afternoon? I need some repair work done right away," Mr. Ramsey said.

"I'm free," I said.

"Great. The whole side of my dock has washed away. I have no idea when it happened. We haven't been up here all summer."

"No one has," I said. "Not with this weather."

"Yes, well, we're here now for two weeks. My family has been looking forward to this for a month. And I won't be able to take them out in the boat until that dock is in some kind of decent shape. I paid a fortune for that damn thing. You'd think it would hold together."

"Not much can hold together in those rains," I said, but he didn't seem to be hearing me. He was thinking.

"How much do you charge?"

"It's negotiable," I said. For people like Tom I charged next to nothing. But it was a different story for a guy like Ramsey. I was willing to hear his offer.

"I'll give you ten plus expenses if you finish before sundown."

"Ten dollars for the whole day?" I asked. I'd heard rich people could be cheap with labor, but this was ridiculous.

"Ten an hour," he said a little impatiently. "But I expect my money's worth."

"You'll get it," I said.

It was shaping up into a good day.

Chapter 3

"Your family have a place up here?" Clark Ramsey asked as we made our way through the path between cabins.

"No, sir. I'm staying over at the Stones' trailer."

"Stones?"

"Bill Stone of Stone Chrysler?" That was Rodney's father's business, a booming car dealership in the middle of town. I thought that might impress Mr. Ramsey, but he seemed genuinely uninterested. Right away I could see he was one of those people who asked questions and never absorbed the answers.

"Crane," he said. "Do I know your father? What line of work is he in?"

"Insurance. But he just died." I hadn't yet come up with a dignified way of saying that.

"That's too bad," he said, as if I'd told him I'd sprained my ankle.

The Ramseys' place appeared in the woods,

a sprawling affair full of big windows and balconies looking out onto the lake. Next to The House it was the nicest one on the cove.

"How well do you know Tom Wheat?" he asked.

"I've known him awhile."

"An interesting guy," he said, but the way he sniffed when he said it made it clear that "interesting" was nothing close to a compliment.

"You're friends with Zan, you said?"

"Not friends. I just know who she is."

He seemed pleased with the distinction. The closer we got to the house, the more conscious I became of my appearance. I was wearing only a pair of ragged cutoffs and a faded blue T-shirt. I never saw the point of dressing up on work days, not that I'd have much to dress up in. I had let my hair go during the summer and it was almost to my shoulders, thick brown waves that didn't look combed even when they were. I hadn't shaved in a while either, though a week's worth of beard on me wasn't much. I was barefoot, too, as always. The skin on the bottom of my feet was as tough as leather, and shoes seemed pointless. But now I found myself wishing I were put together a little better.

I could see people on the screened-in back porch, sitting around in lawn chairs drinking from tall glasses. A faint sound of classical music floated down from that direction. Schubert. You'd never know it to look at me, but I know something about music. I got it from my father.

We bypassed the house and went straight to the dock. Mr. Ramsey didn't say anything as we approached. He didn't need to. I could see the gaping hole in the side of the dock, as if some wild animal had taken a bite out of it.

It was a good dock, a floater. Those always withstood the rains better than stationary docks. I preferred them anyway. They were more versatile and worked better with any kind of boat, especially the speeders. Those bounced around in the water like crazy, and you didn't want them banging up against a stationary force.

"It's not as bad as it looks," I said as I inspected it. Mr. Ramsey stood a few steps back, to be sure the water didn't splash on his clothes. "It's a clean break. I'd just have to replace about a half a dozen boards, all standard size. I should have what you need back at the trailer."

"Good," he said. "So how long will you be?"

"Most of the day. But not more."

He shook hands with me again as I rose, as if it would have been impossible for him to do business otherwise. I couldn't say it was because he seemed to respect me or appeared impressed in any way. His eyes wandered. He was on to other things.

I went back to the trailer and got what I needed, then started to work as the sun was reaching its zenith. I shed my shirt right away, and I could feel the heat on my back, pressing but not penetrating. My skin was too dark, my tan too secure to burn. My body had adapted to the weather.

I had brought my radio with me, as I did on any job, but had neglected to turn it on. Schubert was still drifting down from the cabin. It was the *Unfinished Symphony* now, one of my favorites, and I listened with pleasure, frustrated only by the fact that I couldn't increase the volume.

"Imagine," my father used to say. "This was the piece he was dissatisfied with. Imagine the genius that could move on from this and say, 'I want something better.' "

"Something better" was his Ninth Symphony, a miraculous piece, which was what my father listened to night after night, right before he died. Not that night, though. That night he had a curious lapse. I thought of it and my head swooned. The heat had worked its way to me at last. I thought I heard the sound of wind chimes, pieces of crystal clinking together. It made me dizzy and nostalgic. The wind chimes on our porch. Too many of them. My mother thought they were magic.

"Here, do you want this?" It was a real voice, not my mother's. I jumped and knocked some nails into the lake.

I looked up, and that was the first time I saw Abby. She was standing over me, wearing a red one-piece bathing suit, the sun backlighting her so I couldn't see her features. I could see she was small and thin. Until I caught her face in a shadow, I thought she might be a child. A clearer view changed that. She was my age at least, her face that of a near woman, round and smooth, pretty even in the harsh light.

"I thought you might be thirsty," she said. "You've been out here for hours."

I stood and wiped my hands on my cutoffs, staring directly into her eyes. They were gray-blue, the color of the lake on a misty morning. Her hair was dull blond and short, thin bangs lifting in the breeze. Freckles dotted her nose, faint and feminine, like the markings on a fawn. When she smiled her nose crinkled.

"Thanks," I said, taking the glass from her. It was water, cold, clear, and sweet.

"I'm Abby Winston," she said.

"I'm Tyler Crane."

"Your nose is red, Tyler Crane. You better put some zinc oxide on it."

"It stays this color in the summer. It never peels."

"Lucky you. I always peel. But that's because I'm a city dweller. The sun doesn't agree with me."

I stared into her eyes and I wanted to ask her a thousand questions, but they all jammed up inside me and I could only keep staring, water in one hand, hammer in the other. The sound of Schubert went away and all I could hear was the lake sloshing.

"There you are!" came another voice. "Daddy's beside himself. He wants a game of hearts and he wants it now. No one escapes."

Zan Ramsey was approaching us. She was her usual perfect self, thick black hair tied in a ponytail, long limbs moving gracefully, blue eyes planted in my direction but not on me. They looked beyond, to the water, the cabins across the cove, the sky—anything more engaging than my face. She wore a white bikini. Her body, even when it was nearly exposed, protected itself. It didn't allow you to know its secrets. I could only look at her hairline. It was the safest distance from anything.

"You shouldn't be on the dock. Daddy says it's coming apart," she said to Abby.

"It's perfectly safe," I said, finding my voice. "In another two hours it'll be like new."

"Hmm," she said, then turned to Abby. "Eric just called to apologize to me, but I hung up on him. Did I do the right thing?"

I knew she was talking about Eric Carlisle, one of those all-around-best types that she was practically engaged to on and off. Their break-ups gave every man at school a leap of hope, until it turned out to be a false alarm.

"I don't know, Zan. You ought to just confront him. Don't string him along."

"I'm not stringing. I just want him to know I won't be treated this way. He's too secure, that's his problem. He knows I love him so he treats me like dirt. If I give him a good scare he'll be back on his best behavior. That's how men are."

Abby turned to me with a playful smile. "Is that how men are?"

"You're asking me?"

"You're a man, aren't you?"

"Occasionally."

She laughed. Zan didn't.

"Will we be able to take the boat out tomorrow?" Zan asked me.

"I don't see why not."

"Do I know you?" she asked, squinting her eyes.

"We go to school together."

She stared at me a little harder, trying to place me, then gave up.

"Oh, well. I'm Zan Ramsey. This is my cousin, Abby Winston. She's visiting from D.C."

"Oh, really," I said, trying to think of something to say about D.C. Nothing came to mind, since I'd never been there.

"Her father's in the House," Zan said, "so watch your step."

I looked past her to the cabin. "Oh, is he spying on us?"

"Not that house, idiot," Zan said, laughing. "The House of Representatives. You've heard of it?"

"The U.S. House of Representatives?" I asked. "Yeah, I've heard of it. Isn't it somewhere up north?"

Great move, Crane, I thought. Falling for the daughter of a congressman. Just your league.

"Anyway, Abby, Daddy is serious about this game of hearts. He's dealing you a hand, so don't be late."

Zan moved off then, stepping carefully over stones along the way.

"I wish Zan wouldn't tell people that," Abby said to me. "About my father. It embarrasses them and it's really no big deal."

"It certainly isn't. Especially since my father is the secretary of defense."

She laughed, crinkling her nose.

"I hope I'll see you around. We're here for two weeks. Where are you staying?"

"Right through those woods. You'll see me if you look hard enough."

"I'll look," she said.

Chapter 4

The job took longer than I thought it would. I found some rotted boards underneath, so I had to replace them. I still finished by sundown and did an expert job, if I do say so myself. I figured the dock would probably last through a hurricane.

"Not bad" was all Mr. Ramsey said as he slipped a crisp hundred-dollar bill into my hand.

I stared at it.

"What's wrong?"

"It's too much."

"Ten an hour plus expenses, isn't that what we agreed?"

"It's still too much."

"Never quibble about too much, young man. Only about too little. You've got to learn how to look out for yourself if you want your business to succeed."

I didn't know how to tell him this wasn't a business, just a job. Somehow I figured he'd long ago forgotten the difference. Still, I took his advice and didn't quibble. I needed the bucks, and it was only pride that made me want to act like I didn't.

I said goodbye and walked away, throwing a look over my shoulder at the screened porch. I could see a cluster of people sitting around a long table, but I couldn't pick Abby out. Just as I stepped into the path I heard her laugh behind me, clear, cool, and sweet, like the water she had given to me.

Back at the trailer I took a shower in the tiny bathroom. I barely had room to move and the water came in spurts of hot and cold, but eventually it did the job. When I got out I took a good look in the mirror.

My hair looked longer and more unruly when it was wet. It was my father's hair, thick and wavy. I took some scissors out of the medicine cabinet and started snipping at it, trying to give it some shape. I toweled it dry, gave myself a shave, and stepped back to look at the results. Not bad. Almost respectable, in fact.

I never spent much time wondering if I was good-looking. But that night I did. What did Abby see when she looked at me? Did she even bother to form an opinion?

I couldn't think about it. It was too scary.

But I couldn't stop, either. My mind had been preoccupied with her since the moment I saw her. I urged it on to other things, but it kept jumping back.

"A congressman's daughter," I said aloud, to see if the sound of it was as intimidating as I imagined. It was. I couldn't ignore the facts: she was pretty, she was Zan's cousin, her family had money, and where there was money, there was power.

Because my mother spent so much time worrying about money, putting pressure on my father to make it, implying that we would somehow be different people if we had it, I had made a solemn vow never to worry about getting rich. Recently I had decided I didn't even want to go to college, even though I knew my father had set up a savings fund for that purpose. He wanted me to go to Columbia, where he had gone to law school for two years. "You'll do better than I did," he told me. "You're smarter. You've got more guts." I wasn't sure why he thought that, but he made me believe it. He wanted me to be the success that he never was, and I didn't want to disappoint him. But when he died, it seemed like my reasons for wanting to do great things got buried along with him.

I didn't think it would ever matter that I

wasn't rich, because I had never met any wealthy people that I liked very much. Meeting Abby had changed all that. Now I was worried. Would my lowly social status make a difference to her? Would she expect certain things that I couldn't give? But surely I was jumping ahead of myself. How much money did I need just to talk to her on the dock of her uncle's house?

Still, I kept hearing this nagging voice in my head saying, "A congressman's daughter. And you practically an orphan."

The sound of that made me feel even more scared and a little guilty. I dressed, then went for the phone, dialing my aunt Lena's number.

"What's wrong?" she asked in a hysterical tone. My family was full of overreactors. It was one of the things that drove my dad nuts.

"Everything is an event," he always said. "Nothing can just happen. It has to 'occur.'"

"Nothing, Aunt Lena. I was just calling to check on Mom. Is she okay?"

"Your poor mother. What she has had to endure. It's enough to break anybody's spirit."

"Is she all right?"

"She's as well as you could expect."

"Put Aunt Rhona on." She was the most well-adjusted of my aunts. You could get a straight answer out of her, anyway.

"You just keep yourself out of trouble," Aunt Lena said before she surrendered the phone. "Your mother can't take much more."

"Ty? Where are you?" asked Aunt Rhona.

"I'm at the lake. I'm fine."

"I hate to think of you being all by yourself."

"I'm not. My friend Rod comes up a lot. And I've got neighbors."

"Still, it worries me. Are you sure you wouldn't rather stay with us?"

"I'm fine," I repeated. I couldn't stand the thought of moving in with them. At the moment I couldn't even stand the thought of going back to Flanders.

"Your mother is all right. She has good days and bad days. But we're taking good care of her."

"Maybe she should see a doctor."

"They'd just put her away. She couldn't bear that. And I wouldn't be able to live with myself. She still has you to think about. I keep telling her that."

I didn't say anything. As hard as it was to face, I knew my mother hadn't really thought about me in a long time.

I swallowed hard and said, "Put her on."

"Yes. All right."

I was nervous as I waited. I lit a cigarette

from a pack that Rod had left lying around. He smoked like a chimney, but I hadn't really picked up the habit. The rush to my head made me dizzy.

"Where are you?" came my mother's voice. It was gravelly, as I remembered it, like someone with a bad cold. But that was the way she always talked.

In a patient voice, I explained where I was. I had told her a thousand times.

"You've run away from home," she declared.

"No, Mom. How are you feeling?"

"We never do anything. We never go anywhere."

I took a long drag from the cigarette, holding it in.

"Where do you want to go?" I asked.

"Anywhere. I need to get out. But we can't because we don't have the money."

"I sent you some money."

"It's your father," she said, lowering her voice as if he might hear. "You know he hates to part with a dollar."

"Dad's dead, Mom."

"It's his fault we're poor. He didn't live up to his promise. He should have been a judge by now. He's not a salesman. He never was. He has a good mind. He just gives up too easy."

"Mom, please." But I knew I was asking for something impossible. I was asking her to be whole again.

"So now we're poor and we can't go anywhere. He even makes me pay for my own lunch when we go out."

I pressed the receiver hard against my cheek. The cigarette was making me sick now. I stubbed it out. When I put the receiver against my ear Mom was gone and Aunt Lena was back.

"What did you say to her? She's crying."

"I didn't say anything."

"Hasn't she had enough?"

"Take good care of her, okay?"

"What do you think we're doing?"

"I know. Just . . . just keep her safe."

"Keep yourself safe, young man."

I hung up hard, as if that might sever some connection. But it never went away. Ever, ever.

I ate a bologna sandwich and tried to read. I kept getting up and walking to the window, looking out as if I just wanted to gaze at the lake. But I wanted to see Abby.

No one was on the lake now. The water rolled gently against the shore.

I tried to watch TV. It was an old set and it only picked up two channels. One of them had a baseball game on. I never cared for baseball, or any televised sports. Another thing I got from my father. He said people should concern themselves with intellectual pursuits. *Exercise your mind. Run with it. Make it leap. That's where the power is.*

So why were you listening to baseball the night you died, Dad? Did you just give up on everything?

I switched off the TV and fell asleep on the couch. And I had the dream again.

I'm running all over my house, looking for something. I don't know what it is, I just know I have to have it. I tear the place apart. I know I'll get in trouble, but I don't care—I have to find it. Then I throw open a closet door and there he is, looking the way he looked when I found him. Plaster-white, gray lips, slumped against the window. "Wake up!" I shout. "Wake up!" And in the dream he does. His eyes come open, dark and sad like mine. "Did you think I'd leave you?" he asks, always, and I wake up.

I was sweating and my breath was coming hard and fast. I went to the liquor cabinet and poured myself a glass of brandy. I rarely drink, except for the occasional beer. But after the dream I felt so loose, so disconnected. I felt I needed the taste of something hard and real.

I moved to the window again as I drank the brandy. It was dark out now. A pearl of a moon hung low in the sky. The lake was glistening like a black diamond. I looked at The House, standing tall in the shadows. How could anything so big and beautiful be empty?

But just as that thought flickered across my mind, I saw a light. It popped on suddenly and it made me jump. It was coming from the second floor of The House. I blinked, wondering if I was still dreaming, if the brandy had gotten to me. But the light remained.

Then a silhouette passed in front of it, not once but twice. So it finally has a tenant, I thought. A new neighbor. Maybe someone with a dock in need of repair.

The light went off again and I stared for another second at The House before draining the glass of brandy and surrendering to exhaustion.

Chapter 5

〰〰 I took the Stones' boat out the next morning. I tried to do that a couple of times a week, not only because I enjoyed it, but because it was good for the engine. It was a decent motorboat, a little old but in okay shape. It could pull a couple of skiers without flinching. I learned how to ski on this boat, in fact, and it had remained one of my passions. Skiing always felt a little bit like a miracle to me, like walking on water.

Driving the boat was a different sensation. It was another kind of power. Standing at the wheel, I felt above everything, in control. It was an illusion, I knew, but I enjoyed it anyway.

I slowed the boat down as I passed the Ramseys' place. It looked empty. They had probably taken their boat out first thing. I couldn't help feeling proud when I saw the dock, sturdy and strong from my repairs, bobbing in the water as the waves rolled under it.

I wished I had paid more attention to Abby

when I saw her. I wished I had studied her face. It was already starting to fade a little, lost in my overworked memory and imagination.

I drove up to the dam and back. I had an eerie sort of fascination with the dam. It was the only part of the lake that suggested something sinister. People had died building that dam and rumor was their bodies were still entombed in the concrete. It was bizarre to think anything like that could happen at Flanders Lake.

There was another reason I was drawn to the dam. I knew that every evening, around nine o'clock, they drained some water off the lake. An alarm would sound, and the water would start to be sucked into the dam. Any boats in the vicinity had to leave pretty fast, or they might be sucked into the dam along with the water. Though I'd never been at any risk of that, in fact had never even been near the dam when it was happening, the image haunted me. I used to have nightmares about it, long before I started having the dreams about my father. The idea of getting sucked in, pulled and tugged against my will, into some kind of free-floating, eternal darkness. It was a feeling I sometimes had at home, watching my mother pacing distractedly around the kitchen, wringing her hands and muttering. It was a feeling I had thinking of my father sitting in his chair, staring blankly out the window. Whenever that feeling came to me in real life, I would leave, run as fast and far as I could. When it came to me in a dream I woke up, sweating and gasping for breath.

The dam signified all those things to me—power and mystery and inescapable fate. That was why I was eager to go in that direction, then just as eager to get away. I had to look at it. But I didn't have to like it.

I drove out to the middle of the lake and cut the motor, letting the boat float for a while. I lay in the sun and let my skin absorb it. I listened to the lake sounds—people swimming and skiing, birds shrieking overhead, leaves rustling in the warm breeze. Finally I started back to Bolwood Cove. I had decided to drive past The House and see if the new tenant, whoever he was, needed some dock work.

On my way I became distracted by the sight of some activity on the Ramseys' dock. I slowed the boat down and cast a glance in that direction. I recognized her immediately. She was wearing a different bathing suit, a navy and white bikini. She was leaning up on her elbows, talking to Zan. I waved but they didn't see me. Finally I let the boat drift in their direction.

"How's the dock holding up?" I called out.

Abby got to her feet and waved me toward them.

"It's brilliant," she said. "We have the best dock on the lake."

Zan even smiled at me as I let the boat drift up to the shoreline.

"Daddy's thrilled. We took the boat out this morning. Abby got up on her first go."

"I'd never skied before," she admitted. "It's great, isn't it?"

I just smiled. My imagination hadn't deceived me. If anything, she was prettier than I remembered.

"Climb out and stay awhile," Zan said.

"Well . . ."

"Don't be shy. What else have you got to do?"

"Actually I was just heading over to the house across the cove, see if maybe they need some dock work done."

"What house?" Zan asked, stretching her long tanned legs out in front of her.

"That big one."

"Well, you're out of luck. Nobody's there. It's been empty forever."

"A house like that is empty?" Abby asked. "Who does it belong to?"

"Dr. Kaplan. He's a big-deal surgeon in

Norwood. He built it three summers ago, but he's never used it. The rumor is that he can't afford to keep it up and is looking to sell it. But nobody around here can pay what he's asking."

"If I had a house like that I'd find a way to use it," Abby said, staring at it. I took that opportunity to stare at her. I looked away quickly when I caught Zan turning her eyes to me.

"Well, anyway," I said, "there's somebody there now."

"Says who?" Zan challenged.

"I saw somebody there last night. There was a light on upstairs."

"You must have imagined it."

"No. I saw somebody walking around."

Zan shrugged. "Maybe old Kap has finally moved in."

"Anybody want to take a ride over there?"

"I'll go," Abby volunteered, getting to her feet.

"I won't. I'm waiting for Eric to call."

"Oh, for goodness' sake. Either make up with him or let him go. This is getting ridiculous."

"We're trying to make up. It's a long process."

Abby rolled her eyes at me, and I smiled. I felt like we were sharing a secret joke.

"Well, I'm going. I can't sit in the sun anymore. I'll burn to a crisp."

I helped her into the boat. Her hand felt small and light in mine.

"Have fun," Zan said.

"Uncle Clark won't mind?" Abby asked.

"Uncle Clark is inside making phone calls. Mama is completely stressed. He just can't leave his business alone."

We waved to Zan and I started the boat up, guiding us gently back into the lake. Abby stretched out in the seat beside me, shading her eyes from the sun.

"You cut your hair," she observed.

"Yeah. It was getting out of hand."

"I liked it," she said. Just my luck.

"It'll grow back."

She reached over and touched it. A chill bolted through me.

"It's thick, isn't it?"

"Yeah."

"I wish mine was." She leaned back again, running her fingers through her own light bangs.

"Yours is nice."

She smiled at me and then closed her eyes, offering her face to the sun.

"I like it here, don't you?" she asked.

"Yeah. I wish I lived here."

"I thought you did."

"Only for the summer."

"I'd like to live anywhere besides D.C. Daddy says when he gives up his seat we're moving to Vermont. I'll believe it when I see it."

I wondered what it felt like to be her, but before I could ask she volunteered the information.

"It's lousy being a politician's daughter, you know. Someone is watching your every move. Mama and Daddy practically have to interview my friends. I can't be seen with the 'bad element.'"

"What element is that?"

"Any kind that would get me in the press."

"Like a vagabond dock repairman?"

She laughed. "No, I didn't mean that."

But she had said it.

"I guess that's why I feel comfortable with Zan," she went on, sounding a little flustered. "She has to watch her step, too. Her father's a real big deal in Flanders. Do you know what he does?"

"Yeah, he owns two textile mills."

"And a winery. In fact, that's the only thing he pays any attention to these days. It drives Aunt Muriel insane."

"So there's tension in the home?" I asked.

"Not serious. Just two people stuck together, making each other pay for it."

She smiled when she said all this. Did she really think it was funny? More likely, it wasn't all that accurate. I could show her an unhappy marriage. I could show her two people making each other pay. *Could have.* Past tense.

"Are you okay?" she asked me. I must have gone quiet without knowing it. The cloud of gloom, as Rod called it, had apparently passed over me.

"I'm fine," I said, trying to sound like I meant it.

"I always say the wrong thing."

"No you don't."

People like Abby never said the wrong thing, mainly because they had the right to say anything. Only the rich and crazy had that privilege, my father said.

The House seemed to grow as we approached it. It was twice as big as it appeared from the other side. There was something Gothic about the place. It was brand new but looked ancient, as if it had been there for centuries.

"Bizarre," Abby said as we pulled up to the dock.

I was disappointed to find that the dock was in good shape, a sizeable stationary affair with brand-new weather-treated wood. I thought I might be able to talk them into letting me build them a floater as well. A house this big could use more than one dock, especially if they had more than one boat.

I moored the boat and jumped out, offering my hand to Abby. "Let's explore," I said.

"I think I'll stay here," she said. "I've got a nice view of the place from here, and the sun feels good."

"Okay. I'll only be a minute."

"It looks pretty empty to me," she said as I started up the path.

It was more than empty—it felt hollow. My bare footsteps seemed to echo as I stepped on the porch. I tapped on the door and that echoed, too. I tapped again. Nothing.

I went around to one of the bay windows and peeked in. The place was abandoned. No, not abandoned, since that would imply someone had once lived there. It was *vacant*. No furniture, no pictures, no debris, no indication that a human being had ever been inside those bare walls. Yet I had seen the light. And a shadow.

I moved across the porch and looked in another window. This room was enormous, with

bleached wood floors that must have cost a fortune. A crystal chandelier hung overhead, the
sunlight catching on the facets. But this room
was not empty. Two objects inhabited it. One
was a crate, over in a far corner, marked This
End Up. And the other, looking as out of place
as anything could, was a telephone. It was the
old kind, black, with a rotary dial. I was sure it
wasn't functional. Who would have put it there?

"There's nobody home!" came Abby's voice
from the boat. "And if there is, you'll get arrested for trespassing!"

"And your name would be dragged through
the mud," I called back. She laughed, and I
turned to look at her.

"Come on, Tyler. I'm starting to blister."

"You're the one who—"

I didn't finish my sentence, because a sudden, jarring sound interrupted me. It was the
phone ringing. I whirled around and looked
back in the window. It was definitely coming
from that room. I stood and waited for someone
to answer it. No one did. It rang about half a
dozen times, then stopped.

"I'm counting to ten, then I'm firing this
baby up," Abby called.

"I'm coming."

I walked back down the path, my mind

buzzing. So a phone rang in an empty house. Was that a big deal? I wondered if I should tell Abby about it, but I decided against it. I didn't want her to think I was overly dramatic.

Your nerves are on edge, boy, I reminded myself. They have been since June. It'll take a while to recover.

I walked back to the boat and made myself smile at Abby, even as I wondered:

Who put the phone there? Who would be calling?

And who did they think would answer?

Chapter 6

"This is cozy," Abby said, strolling through the trailer, which was really only a matter of taking a couple of ninety-degree turns.

"Is that a tactful way of saying it's a dump?"

"No. That would be 'it has character.'"

She sat down on the couch and spread her arms across the back, still looking around the room for a conversation piece.

"Is that your family?" she asked, nodding at a picture of Rod and his parents standing on the dock, smiling in the sunlight. It was about three years old; that was how long it had been since the Stones had come up here.

"No. That's the family who owns this place."

"Oh, right. I forgot."

"Want something to drink?" I asked, hoping to head off any questions about my family.

"Sure. A Coke or something."

I was still reeling from the fact that Abby

was here with me, in the trailer. Not that I could give myself any of the credit; she was the one who'd suggested it after we left The House. Everything was pointing to the fact that she was interested in me. Still, I had trouble believing it.

I was suddenly very conscious of the condition of the trailer—the dull carpet, the worn furniture, the lack of regard for the kind of luxuries which were present in Clark Ramsey's lake house. I wanted to apologize for everything, which was especially ridiculous since I wasn't responsible for any of it.

I walked back into the living room and handed Abby a glass as I sat on the couch beside her, keeping a respectable distance.

"So your parents don't mind you living up here?" she asked.

"No," I answered evasively.

"Mine would freak. But I guess it's different with girls."

"I guess."

I groped around in my brain for a quick change of subject, but I wasn't fast enough.

"What does your father do?" she asked.

I didn't want to say it. I was tired of hearing it, tired of finding new and dignified ways of repeating it, tired of the various reactions. Shock, sympathy, indifference. Each was painful in its own way.

I kept silent a long time, staring at the ice cubes in my glass, contemplating a lie that wouldn't come.

"I'm sorry. Is that a bad subject?" she asked.

"Yeah."

"Me and my mouth," she said. "There I go again."

I smiled at her. She was watching me with a concerned expression. Her face was so pure and sweet, as if it had never even witnessed a bad intention. Maybe it was time for me to stop being so cynical. People with money couldn't help it, could they? Maybe they even had problems, though at the moment it was hard for me to think of what they could be.

Abby bit her bottom lip and ran her fingers through her hair.

"Next category, please," she said, mimicking a game show host. I laughed.

"I could tell you. It's just that it's so hard for people to hear."

"He's dead," she said.

"Uh-huh."

"I'm sorry."

"Me too."

She put a hand on my arm; it was cool and light. "When?"

"June."

"Is that all you want to say about it?"

"I guess." But I had my doubts. Maybe that was the problem. Maybe I had talked about it too little, not too much.

"No," I said quickly. "I want to tell you."

She nodded, moving closer to me, wrapping her hands around one of her knees and pulling it to her chest. She waited, but I didn't know how to start.

"What did he die of?" she asked.

"Heart failure."

She was waiting for more, and I found I wanted to tell her.

"He should have been a lawyer," I said. "He had a great mind. He was this kid from a poor family in Hungary. He was smuggled into the country when he was only about six and raised by a distant aunt. He worked his way through college loading coal onto a train. He made it into law school, and he did well for the first year. And then, somehow, something gave out. His money. His spirit. Something. Anyway, he quit. He ended up selling insurance. And he was lousy at it. His heart wasn't in it. His talents were wasted."

"That's the saddest thing in the world—a wasted talent," Abby said.

"So he spent his whole life feeling like a failure. He knew it but wouldn't say it. Even though my mother was constantly reminding him of it."

I took a breath. It was getting more difficult. But I looked at Abby and she was listening—not out of sympathy or politeness, but because she wanted to know.

"The thing is, he put all his hopes in me. He never really said it, but I knew. He was constantly teaching me things, little bits of information. Like, '1066, the Norman invasion. Harold took an arrow in the eye.' Or 'Beethoven's Third Symphony, the *Eroica*—changed the face of classical music.' He wanted me to know stuff. He wanted me to have a jump on everybody else."

"Did that bother you? I mean, that he put pressure on you?"

I shook my head. "It didn't feel like pressure. It just felt like he had faith in me. And I was glad, because my mother never did."

"Why not?"

I shrugged. "My mother is . . . different."

It was harder to talk about her.

"Anyway," I said, taking a needed breath, "I

relied on my father in a big way. I never really realized how much."

"Were you there?" Abby asked gently. I looked at her. "When he had the heart attack?"

"No. No. Nothing attacked him. It failed. *He* failed. He bailed out."

I saw her shrinking away from me a little, surprised by my anger.

"He had no right to do it. To leave me alone with her. He had no right. None."

I was on my feet now, clenching my fists. I had felt this way a long time but had never said it.

"Come on, Tyler," she said softly. "It's not like he wanted to die."

I turned around and glared at her, wanting to say something hateful. She caught the look and let her eyes wander.

A thick silence fell between us. I wanted to do something to save the afternoon, but I felt helpless. Why did my father keep coming back? Why couldn't he stay dead?

"I'm sorry I brought it up," Abby said.

"No, it's my fault."

She shrugged and scratched her shin lightly. The motion comforted me. It seemed real and logical.

"Do you play backgammon?" I suddenly asked.

"Not if I can avoid it."

"You can't," I said, and went for the set.

We played for the rest of the afternoon, refilling our glasses of Coke, turning on lights when the sun started to get weak. It was soothing, the sound of dice rolling across the felt, the clack of tokens moving around the board, Abby making little humming sounds as she contemplated her moves. I watched her face as she thought. I wanted a clearer picture, something to hold on to. I was afraid of never seeing her again.

Once when I got up for more ice, I paused by the window to look out at The House. It was dark and empty. Nothing moved in or around it. I stared at it and thought about the telephone ringing in the empty room.

Suddenly there was a real ringing sound, and I nearly jumped out the window. The phone in the trailer was ringing. I could only stare at it, as if it might attack me.

"Want me to get that?" Abby asked.

I nodded wordlessly.

"Hello? . . . This is me, Uncle Clark," she said. "I'm over at Tyler's place. . . . It's just through the woods, practically next door. . . .

But Zan knew where I was," she said, trying to lower her voice, turning away from me. "Yes, we went over there, but then we came back here. . . . I'm sorry you were worried. . . . I'll be home soon. . . . Bye."

She hung up and gave me an apologetic look.

"He doesn't like you being here," I said.

"He feels responsible for me."

Neither of us said what we were both thinking: he might not have been so worried if I were someone else.

"I'll take you back in the rowboat."

"That's okay," she said. "I can walk."

"I insist. I'm a gentleman. I don't want Uncle Clark to worry. It's not good for his skin."

"You're cruel," she said, giving me a swift, soft kiss on the cheek. "I'm a big girl, though. I can take care of myself."

I stood there watching her walk quickly away until she disappeared into the shadows. Staring into the darkness, I wondered how Clark Ramsey knew my telephone number.

Chapter 7

⹀⹀ After Abby left, I went back into the trailer with every intention of thinking about her and our day together. But before I knew it, I was thinking about the night my father died.

The house had been too quiet. I couldn't find our dog, Sport, and I knew how upset my father would be if anything happened to him. Somewhere in the distance a radio hummed. I followed it. I saw the door and I knew something was wrong before I walked in.

The telephone. I picked it up. *Dial 911.* In the background my mother shouting. *Dial 911.* No, she is saying something else. "I wish it was me!" Shut up, I'm screaming at her. *911.*

"I think my father is dead."

"Do you need an ambulance, sir?"

"I . . . no. I don't think so. I'm pretty sure he's dead."

"We'll send an ambulance. I just need your address."

"I wish it was me!" she is screaming.

Why is she saying that? She's not. She's saying something else.

At the funeral, all those people watching, listening, she throws herself on the casket, knocking the flowers to the ground. She points at me and shouts. Her voice is gravelly. She points and shouts, "You wish it was me! You wish it was me!"

I look away. Everyone is staring. Something comes down around me like cold, hard steel. I focus on a blade of grass curling across my shoe. They are watching me, waiting for an answer, a denial that I can't give.

I do wish it. I do.

≡

I sat for a long time in the darkness, staring at nothing. The nights were always the worst part. Sometimes I wished I lived somewhere that the daylight never went away. I looked out the window at The House. There were no lights on. But I couldn't help thinking that someone was there.

I went outside, down to the dock, pounding the ground with a stick as I walked to keep the snakes away. It was late in the year for them, but I never took chances.

This was often my remedy for insomnia. I went down and sat in the boat until I began to feel sleepy. It didn't take long, with the water sloshing and the night birds cooing and the boat rocking back and forth. The rowboat was better than the motorboat. It put you closer to the water.

I sat back and stared up at the stars as the boat bobbed up and down. I was already starting to feel relaxed. The memories were slipping away. My eyes were feeling heavy.

Then I saw it, out of the corner of my eye. A light, tiny and quick, coming from behind the trees. Across the cove, next to The House. Not in it, beside it. I sat up quickly and grabbed an oar, as if to protect myself. The light flickered once more, then went away. If I weren't a sensible man, I would have sworn it was a ghost.

I sat there for a long moment, wondering what to do. Then, without even asking myself why, I began to row in the direction of the light.

The distance was longer than it appeared. Halfway across I began to feel tired. But some crazy desire, something between curiosity and obsession, was moving me on. I couldn't have turned back if I wanted to.

I tied my boat to the dock and climbed out. I still had my stick with me, but no flashlight. The moon was full, but a film of clouds had moved across it, making everything hazy. I pounded the ground lightly as I made my way up the path, careful not to make myself heard.

This is stupid, I thought as I approached the porch. So what if I saw a light? So what if there's a telephone inside? Someone owns this place. They have a right to come here. It's no big deal.

I suddenly felt silly, even hysterical, like my mother's side of the family. My dad would have accused me of overreacting. It was a hereditary trait. But I was listening to a stronger side, something that I got from him: instinct. An ability to know it, in my gut, when something wasn't quite right. That instinct took me around the side of The House, to the place where I thought I had seen the light. Nothing was there but trees and brambles.

I made one full circle, looking for any kind of clue. The House was still and dark. I walked up onto the porch and looked around for footprints. None, except my own, following me. The dirt was still damp from the previous rains; no one could have gotten onto the porch without making a print. Unless they had made it a point not to leave a print. Unless they had covered their tracks.

"Ridiculous," I muttered, just to hear the sound of my voice. I was beginning to spook myself.

I turned to go, but something made me look inside one last time, to be sure I'd really seen a telephone in there. Pressing my face against the glass, I saw that it was there. It hadn't been moved since I'd seen it. Nothing had changed. Except . . .

I didn't complete that thought. The sound of a twig snapping made me jump back.

"Who's there?" I asked. Nothing but the wind answered.

I started down the path toward the dock, moving carefully but quickly. I was halfway there, starting to feel a little foolish, when it happened. I felt an arm hook around my neck. It caught me by surprise and jerked me back. My feet came off the ground. I could barely breathe. The grip tightened and all my breath was gone. I strained for air but none came. With all the strength I had left I buried my elbow into the person's ribs. He gave way a little, enough for me to get my breath, and then I waved my stick over me, bringing it down as hard as I could on his head.

He let out a shriek, then everything went quiet. The arm fell away from my throat. I took a couple of deep breaths, then began to run. I jumped in the boat, still gulping in the air, and I began to row with a strength I wouldn't have thought I had left in me. I didn't slow down until I was halfway across the lake, and all was still, and nothing was following me but the moon.

Chapter 8

The next morning I was slightly dazed. If it hadn't been for the pain in my neck, I would have sworn I had dreamed it all. Then, as I was sitting down to breakfast, pouring milk on my cornflakes, it suddenly came to me: the crate.

That was what had been different about the room—the crate marked This End Up was missing. I was sure I had seen it the first time. I remembered wondering if it had something in it, or if it was a substitute for a chair. Had the person who tried to kill me taken it away? Was he looking for it?

But what could be in it that was worth killing somebody for?

A knock at the door made me jump.

"Who is it?" I asked, reaching for a bread knife from the kitchen counter.

"The FBI, the CIA, and the IRS. Are you decent?"

I let out a sigh and went to the door. Abby

looked beautiful in a white outfit, her hair shining in the sunlight. Her eyes were a deeper gray blue than I remembered, like rain clouds, and they were prettier than anything I had ever seen in my life.

"I'm glad to see you," I said.

"I'm glad to see you, too. What happened?" she asked, touching my neck with her fingertips.

"Oh, that." I had woken up to a circle of bruises around my throat, like a plum-colored necklace.

"I fell."

"You fell on your neck?"

"In the shower. It was a complicated situation."

"Mmm. I wish I could have seen it."

I felt myself blush. She just smiled, looking me square in the eye.

"Have you had breakfast?" I asked.

"Yep. Do you want to come sunbathe with us? Uncle Clark isn't taking the boat out today. He's got some important business."

"He's supposed to be on vacation."

"I know, but someone broke into his winery last night and made off with some loot. So Uncle Clark's all upset, and Aunt Muriel doesn't help matters. She keeps going after him, making all these cracks, like, 'At least they broke into the

60

one business that isn't profitable. Maybe we can write it off our taxes.' Good old Aunt M."

I thought of the way my mother nagged my father, wanting him to do better, calling him the dreaded F-word. Failure. As if he didn't know it.

"I wonder if I'll do that to my husband," Abby pondered.

"No. You won't."

"You're right. Because I'll never get married."

"Yes you will."

"What makes you say that?"

"Because people like you do."

She flinched.

"What does that mean? 'People like you.' "

"Never mind."

"No, I want to know. People with short blond hair? People whose names begin with A? People with fair skin?"

"People whose fathers have money and power," I snapped.

It took me a long time to meet her eyes, but when I did they were just as cool and unwavering as ever. If I had hurt her, she wasn't showing it.

"My father's a hardworking person who's trying to help his country."

"Just drop it, okay?"

"I'd love to."

Our eyes met, and I asked myself, what kind of jerk are you? You're crazy about this girl, and you're doing your best to push her away. Is this psychotic or what? I wanted to reach out to her, but I couldn't.

"Do you want to sunbathe or not?" she asked, her voice as cool as her eyes.

"Abby, I'm sorry."

She shrugged. She wasn't going to make it easy on me.

"I have to change my clothes."

"That's not all you have to change," she said, but she was smiling. I started away and she said, "By the way, you can put the knife down. I won't hurt you."

I blushed and tossed it over on the kitchen table.

I quickly changed into my swimming trunks and we left. As we walked along the path, Abby slipped her hand in mine, curling her fingers around it.

"So tell me the problem," she said.

"I've got a lot on my mind."

"What did you do last night?"

I swallowed hard. My throat was still sore.

"Not much," I said.

"I get the feeling you're not telling me the truth."

I looked at her, wondering if I should reveal anything.

"Did you entertain some woman after I went home?"

"No."

"I thought maybe you might call me."

"I don't know your number."

"I thought you might ask."

Suddenly I stopped and turned to her. She stopped, too, with a questioning look.

"Abby, don't do this to me unless you mean it."

"What? Mean what?"

"Don't flirt with me. Don't kid around. I like you a lot. I need to be able to trust you."

She stared at me, unsmiling.

"What makes you think you can't?"

"I'm just not sure . . ." Why in the world you'd be interested in me, I wanted to say, but wisely refrained. "I know everything's happening pretty quick. But I have to know it's real," I said.

She squeezed my hand.

"It's real."

I took a breath, trying to put my thoughts in order.

"Last night I went across the cove—" I started to explain.

"Hello!" came a sudden, booming voice. "Just who I wanted to see!"

We both looked up. Tom Wheat was leaning over his sundeck, waving at us.

"Thank God, I've been saved from myself. Come in and sit a spell!"

Abby and I made our way up to Tom's deck. He had something resembling an office set up out there—a table with a portable typewriter, a collection of reference books, a thermos of coffee, and a portable telephone.

"I'm glad someone decided to visit me," Tom said, pouring us some coffee. "The muses certainly haven't."

I introduced Tom to Abby and he made a big show of bowing to her and kissing her hand.

"I was observing you from above. Spry young lovers frolicking in the wood. It was enough to make me believe in romance all over again."

Abby and I avoided looking at each other. Tom reached under the desk and pulled out a pint of Irish whiskey, then added a dollop to his coffee.

"I love the lake in the morning," he said, taking a breath of air. "The nights here are gloomy. I see things that aren't there. I'm not sure if that's age or too much solitude."

"What are you writing?" Abby inquired, leaning forward to glance at the paper in his typewriter.

"At the moment I am writing the most inspired grocery list ever to pass through a typewriter." He ripped the paper out and set it aside. "But the rest of the time I am simply staring at blank pages and begging a novel to come forth."

"What things do you see?" I asked Tom.

"Things? Ghosts, I suppose."

"What kind of ghosts?"

"Oh, from my past. My future. Things I have done, but mostly things I have not done and, sadly, will never do." He took a long swig of coffee.

"You're still young enough to do lots of things," Abby said.

He smiled at her. "My God. All this and optimism, too."

"But not real ghosts," I persisted.

"Oh, I assure you they are real enough."

"Have you ever seen anything across the cove? Lights in the trees?"

Tom turned a steady gaze on me. "I can't say I have."

"Have you?" asked Abby, as if she thought I was joking.

"Yes," I said. "But they aren't ghosts. They're real."

"Oh, you mean the light in the house," Abby said. "Zan mentioned that to Uncle Clark at dinner the other night. He said you were wrong. Nobody lives there. And nobody's moving in, either."

"I didn't say anyone was living there." I paused, considering it. "And how does he know?"

"He knows the guy who owns it. Dr. Kaplan. He says Kap is in the Bahamas right now."

"I thought we were talking about ghosts," Tom said. "I'm not interested in gossiping about real people."

"We have to be going anyway," Abby said. "Zan will be wondering where we are."

"You are cruel," Tom said as we started away. "If you go I'll be forced to face writing."

"It'll be good for you," I said.

Once we were down the steps and out of earshot Abby said, "He's a strange guy."

"He's all right. He's just lonely."

"He drinks too much."

"Everybody has a vice," I said.

"What's yours?" she asked.

"I wouldn't know where to start."

She laughed, but I didn't. We were quiet for a moment, then Abby said, "Are you actually worried about that light you say you saw? Is that what all this serious stuff is about?"

"Never mind. It doesn't seem so serious anymore."

I had been trespassing; someone had tried to scare me off. They'd probably thought I was an intruder, and were probably just as frightened as I had been. There were still a lot of unexplained things, but I was losing interest. The sun was out, the lake was sparkling, and Abby had her hand in mine. Nothing else mattered.

Chapter 9

⟨≈⟩ Abby, Zan, and I sat on the dock for the rest of the afternoon, soaking in the sun and listening to the radio. Occasionally they amused me with stories from their childhoods. Mostly they recounted family vacations—trips to the Greek islands, Hawaii, ski vacations in Aspen. I sat and listened, having no such adventures to contribute.

"You must have done something fun as a kid," Zan challenged. "Didn't you even go to camp?"

"Don't embarrass him," Abby said.

"No. I stayed at home mostly, in my room, reading books and listening to music."

"Boring," Zan said with a yawn.

"I don't think so," Abby said, defending me.

"Zan has a right to her opinion. She thinks I've had a boring life."

"I guess I'm just the restless type," Zan said, tossing her head back and letting her long black hair cascade behind her. "I need a lot of stimulation."

"Ha, that's a laugh," Abby said, shaking her head. "All you've done is sit here and wait for Eric to call."

"Eric can be very stimulating," Zan answered tartly.

Eventually the sun crept behind the clouds, painting everything in shades of pink and pastel blue. I sat next to Abby, my knee barely touching hers, and watched the birds circling low over the lake as I thought about all the small things in life that could somehow make the bad stuff go away. Abby would probably have been surprised to hear me be so positive. I surprised myself. But it was becoming clear to me why I'd been so unpleasant lately: because I couldn't believe my good fortune. I couldn't believe I could have this so soon after losing my father, this feeling that somebody really cared about me. My disbelief made me want to test it.

"Girls, you'd better get washed up," said Clark Ramsey, walking onto the dock. He was looking as dapper as ever in white pants and a navy pullover. "Dinner will be on the table soon."

I scrambled to my feet and pulled my T-shirt over my head.

"I'd better head back," I said.

"Don't go," Abby said. "Can't you stay for dinner?"

"No, I've got things to do."

"You're perfectly welcome," Ramsey said in a cool voice. "There's more than enough."

"But I'm not dressed right," I said.

"Don't be stupid," said Zan. "This is the lake. We're all slumming it. Daddy insists on everything being ultracasual here. Right, Daddy?"

"That's right."

"Well, if you're sure it's okay."

"I never make an offer unless I'm sure," he said.

Zan and Abby darted up the path toward the house and I was left to walk beside Mr. Ramsey.

"I hope you're not kosher," he said. "We're having pork chops."

"I'm not even Jewish," I said.

He raised an eyebrow at me.

"Well, I mean, my father is. Was. But my mother isn't, so I'm not sure what religion that makes me. But he was never kosher anyway. My father, I mean."

He nodded, smiling an odd smile, maybe because I was babbling. But something told me it was because he thought I was lying.

All the way up to the house, and for moments after I sat down at the table inside the screened porch, I wondered what had made Ramsey assume I was Jewish. He was clearly the definition of a WASP, which probably meant he thought Jews were fine to fix your dock, but not to date your relatives.

Maybe he wasn't assuming. Maybe Clark Ramsey was checking into my background, for Abby's sake.

I tried hard to put these thoughts away and concentrate on dinner. Zan's mother was an older, more sophisticated version of Zan. Muriel Ramsey was a supreme hostess, filling any lulls in conversation with witty little tales she had heard through the grapevine, involving prominent families in town. She behaved as if she were entertaining a party of twelve instead of her family and the local dock repairman.

"The Harstons actually pay off the garbageman," she told us. "They slip him an extra twenty dollars a month and he comes into the house and collects their kitchen trash."

"Rubbish," said Mr. Ramsey, and everyone howled with laughter.

"It's true," she insisted, not so much missing

the joke as choosing to ignore it. "I heard it from a very reliable source."

"Second hair dryer from the left?" Ramsey inquired, and we laughed some more. Uncle Clark was clearly the ruler of this roost. Muriel Ramsey and Zan watched him as if their contentment depended on his, and as if his contentment was not something that could always be counted on. Abby spent a lot of time giving me gentle little jabs under the table, or lightly pinching my kneecaps. I struggled to keep a straight face. I knew that even for me, there was no escaping the powerful eye of Clark Ramsey.

Muriel, on the other hand, hardly looked at me. You might think this made me relax, but it had the opposite effect. I knew what her not looking at me meant. When she didn't look at me, didn't hear me ask for the salt, and had no reaction to my complimenting the food, Muriel Ramsey was reminding me that as far as she was concerned, I didn't exist.

Abby would probably have accused me of making snap judgments, and she'd probably have been right. Would I have been so hard on Muriel if I hadn't known she was rich? It was an impossible question to answer, since in her own sly way, Muriel never let anyone forget she was rich.

Toward the end of the meal, when everyone was looking a little tired, I took advantage of a lull to impress the Ramseys for Abby's sake.

"This is an excellent wine," I said, lifting my glass in the direction of Mr. Ramsey. You wouldn't know it to look at me, but I know wine. My father educated me on it. Whenever we had wine at dinner he made me assess the taste. "You may be called on to do this in public one day," he would say, only half-teasing.

"You like it, do you?" Ramsey asked.

Muriel Ramsey rolled her eyes. She turned toward me and almost as a warning said, "Don't get him started."

"What do you like about it?" Ramsey inquired, ignoring his wife.

"It's full-bodied. It has a lot of wood in it."

Abby giggled. "Are you making this up?"

"That depends on how I'm doing."

Mr. Ramsey smiled. "You're doing quite well."

Mrs. Ramsey interrupted. "Yes, you're doing very well. Now we get to hear *why* it's got so much wood in it."

"My wife grows impatient with my profession."

"It's not a profession. Professionals make

73

money. This *hobby* of yours loses it at a steady pace. And don't forget whose money it is."

There was an awful silence which I quickly filled.

"This is from your winery?" I asked.

He smiled.

"Well, it's really good," I said, turning the bottle around to look at the label. It had a picture of a sailboat against a setting sun, a minimalist-type charcoal sketch. Very tasteful.

"Would you like to know the secret?" he inquired of me.

"Only if you want to tell me."

Suddenly everyone at the table said in unison, "It's the bottle."

"Excuse me?"

Mr. Ramsey picked up the bottle, which was almost empty, and ran his finger along the base of it.

"Most bottles have a solid bottom," he said. "Some of them have an arch here so that the sediment will settle away from the wine. But the problem is, during the settling process, a lot of the flavor of the wine comes to the bottom."

I nodded, following his reasoning, but not sure where it was going.

"My bottle is different. There is a small space between the base and the bottle. A natural air pocket, if you will. This allows a constant molecular movement to occur between the base and the contents. The wine stabilizes. It doesn't settle until you pour it."

"So more of the flavor stays in the body of the wine."

"Exactly," he said, putting the bottle down as if settling a fine but important point.

"And that," said Muriel Ramsey, "is why this wine is so delicious that almost nobody wants to buy it."

"This is a labor of love. I don't mind losing money on it."

"No one minds losing money when it isn't their own," she said.

"Not this," Zan said, rolling her eyes. "The old whose-money-is-it-anyway argument. Really, could you two switch channels for a while?"

Muriel stood. "Dinner is over. Zan, you and Abby and your guest may leave the table."

Before we could, she started in on Clark again. "And you, I repeat, did not earn the money you are now so lavishly losing. It's still my father's."

"I've spent the best years of my life bailing water out of two sinking ships, Muriel. I saved those mills. I've done and will continue to do whatever it takes to keep them going."

Muriel Ramsey said nothing to that. We were still sitting at the table. A feeling of familiarity swept over me. This atmosphere was so familiar, in fact, it almost felt comfortable. It was the rich people's version of the fight my parents always had. Muriel Ramsey had used the F-word. She had called her husband a failure.

Clark Ramsey stared hard at the wine bottle, as if gazing at a lost lover. Under the table I felt Abby's hand on my leg, giving it a reassuring squeeze.

"This wine will make money," he said in a low, even voice, as if his saying it would make it so.

I left around midnight. I walked back through the woods, thinking of how Abby had squeezed my hand under the table and touched the small of my back when she was saying good night to me. I still hadn't kissed her, and I felt the ache of wanting to. Maybe tomorrow. The days were moving too fast.

I thought about dropping by Tom's, but his lights were off. The night was still and quiet. Nothing moved, not even the leaves. I felt like the only thing alive. Yet as I walked along, I began to have the sensation that I was being followed. I stopped and listened. Something rustled far off. Or maybe close by. Sounds could get distorted next to the water.

I started to walk faster. I couldn't tell if I was making the noise or not. I just kept moving; my breath came fast, from somewhere deep, so loud it made me dizzy.

When I got close to the trailer I began to run. I lunged for the doorknob, fumbling in my pocket for the key. I cursed myself for having locked the door before I left. But the knob turned easily and I went inside, slamming the door behind me.

Why wasn't the door locked? I distinctly remembered doing it. I was always careful about that.

Something moved. I fumbled to put the chain on the door, then realized the noise wasn't coming from outside. It was in the trailer. With me.

Slowly I made my way across the room, groping in the darkness for the bread knife. I remembered tossing it on the table that morning. But as my hand roamed across the Formica, it came up with nothing but a salt shaker.

The noise was louder now, more distinct. It was footsteps, moving steadily in my direction. I thrust the salt shaker out in front of me.

"I've got a gun," I said. "And I'll use it."

A light popped on. I stood face-to-face with my assailant.

"Please," Rod said. "Don't salt me."

Chapter 10

"Let me get this straight. Since the last time I was here, you've fallen in love with a senator's daughter, nearly gotten yourself killed, and uncovered a spy ring across the cove."

Rod was lying on the dock, smoking a cigarette and staring up at the stars. I was sitting beside him, taking deep breaths of night air and trying to calm my nerves.

"She's a representative's daughter," I corrected him, "and I don't know if it's a spy ring or what. I just know something strange is going on over there."

"The doc is in the Bahamas, they say?"

"They say."

"So did it dawn on you it could be a bunch of kids? Vandals? A homeless person or two?"

"No. There would be a mess, trash, some kind of debris. The place is spotless."

"Very clean homeless people?"

"And vandals and homeless people wouldn't install a telephone."

"Clean homeless people with lots of relatives?"

"This isn't funny," I said.

"I know it isn't," he said, raising up on his elbows, running his fingers through his bangs. He had the kind of hair I wanted—straight, obedient, blond. Girls went blurry-eyed when they saw him coming; they bumped into things and giggled and punched each other's ribs. His lazy brown eyes gave him the appearance that he didn't care about anything, which made him even more attractive. I dreaded Abby's meeting him.

Would Uncle Clark find Rod a more suitable companion for his niece? I doubted it. We were both out of her class. Rod's father was rich, but he had made his money in an undignified way, by placing tacky ads on TV and staying open until midnight.

"Listen," Rod said, "do you think maybe you're just a little nervous?"

"Why?"

"Because of your dad and all."

"No, Rod."

"It's just a suggestion."

"Do you think I haven't considered that?

Okay, so I'm still bugged about my dad. I still think about it. . . ."

"You still having dreams?"

"Yeah, some. But I'm not imagining this stuff. I'm not going off the deep end, if that's what you're saying."

"It's not."

"I know mental illness runs in my family, but I hear it skips a generation."

Rod gave me a hard look which I knew I deserved. He let me stew for a moment, then said, "You finished?"

"Yeah. Sorry."

He dropped his cigarette into his empty beer can.

"If this is bugging you so much, why don't you just take off?"

"I can't."

"You always have before."

He was referring to the days, not very long ago, when I used to run away from home at regular intervals. Whenever things got tough at home, or simply when the spirit moved me, I'd pack a few things and just duck out. Sometimes I'd go to Rod's house; sometimes I'd just wander around for days, until I could face going back there. My mother called it my disappearing act. "I don't do that anymore," I said.

"Since when?"

"Since now. I want to see something through for once, even if it's something as stupid as this."

I didn't tell him that the biggest reason was Abby. I would be here as long as she was. No force on earth could move me.

He thought for a moment, then said, "Well, we'd better go over there and take a look."

"No. Let's wait till daylight."

He rolled his eyes. "Don't tell me they're vampires."

"I just think it's safer. Nobody's over there then. We could get inside, have a look around."

"Great. Breaking and entering. 'What I Did During Summer Vacation.'"

"You don't have to go along if you don't want to."

"I've been doing stupid things with you since I was six. Why stop now?"

We started up to the trailer and he threw an arm over my shoulder.

"What I'm really interested in is this senator's daughter."

"Congressman," I said. "And it's private."

"In other words, nothing's happened."

I laughed, feeling brave, as if everything

were back to normal. Or as normal as things ever got for me.

＝＝＝

The next morning we got up as the sun was rising and took the motorboat out. Nothing was stirring on the lake except some old fishermen far up on the other end of the cove. Rod kept the engine low and quiet, then cut it as we approached the opposite shore and let us drift up to the dock.

"What do you think?" I asked as he gazed up at The House.

"It's a little extreme, isn't it?"

As we walked up the path I looked for signs of the struggle I had had there, some little piece of evidence. But everything looked perfectly in order, like a house that had never been lived in.

We circled it a couple of times, looking for the easiest way in. We finally settled on a small window in the kitchen. Rod wrapped his T-shirt around a rock, then smashed in the bottom of the pane. As I waited for him to open it, something caught my eye.

"Look at this," I said, bending down, running my hand across the red dirt.

"Paint me a picture," he said, his arm half-way inside the window, groping for the lock.

"Tire tracks," I said. "They're pretty fresh."

"Doesn't mean anything."

"Don't you ever watch detective movies? Everything means something."

Rod finally got the window open and crawled in. I followed him. The kitchen was huge, light and airy, with brand-new tiles and appliances that looked as if they'd never been used. Rod turned on the sink; it sputtered and some brownish water came out.

"Hasn't been turned on in ages," he said, "if ever."

Every room in the house was empty. It had that vacant smell that new buildings have, all hardware and wood and paint, nothing human.

The phone was in the middle of what looked to be the living room. I picked it up and a dial tone buzzed in my ear.

"Why pay for a telephone line if you're not going to use it?" I asked.

"Maybe he used it. To talk to the contractors while they were building the place."

"But it's built. There aren't any more contractors to talk to."

"Look, Ty. I've listened to your story, I've looked around this place, and I've come to the conclusion that there's nothing weird going on here. So you saw a light, so you heard a phone . . ."

"So someone tried to strangle me."

"For trying to break into the house."

"I wasn't—"

"There isn't anything here!"

I slammed the receiver down angrily. "Then why have a phone?"

Rod just stared at me.

"Fine. I'm crazy."

"I didn't say that. You keep saying that. Can we just get out of here? I don't want to get arrested."

"Let's go," I said.

I still don't know what made me do it. It was something like a gut instinct, maybe even a quiet voice. *Try the closet. Just try it.*

I walked toward an ordinary-looking closet next to the stairs. A big bleached pine door with a brass knob. I turned it and nothing happened.

"Locked," I said.

"Don't start," Rod sighed.

"Why would it be locked?"

"Why wouldn't it?"

"Because nothing is in it. The place is empty."

As Rod stood by impatiently, I started working on the lock with my pocketknife. The door was expensive, but fortunately the lock wasn't. I jimmied it after a couple of tries.

I opened the door eagerly and Rod gave a melodramatic gasp.

"Oh my God!" he said, looking inside. "Crates!"

I wasn't laughing, though. They were identical to the crate I had seen in the corner. Plain, wooden, with This End Up stenciled in red. There were about two dozen of them, maybe more. I reached in and dragged one out into the room. It was pretty heavy, but manageable.

"Let's see what's inside," I said, prying it open with the knife.

"Nuclear detonators, no doubt," Rod said. "Being smuggled out to Libyan terrorists."

The top came open and we looked at the contents. Rod started laughing.

"Your criminals are winos," he said, taking out a bottle of wine and holding it up in the light. "Ah, 1989. An excellent year."

"Let me see that," I said, snatching it out of his hands.

"This was a good move after all," Rod was saying behind me. "Let's take one of these for a souvenir."

But I wasn't listening to him. I was busy staring at the label, the sailboat and the setting sun in a charcoal sketch, understated and severe, like Clark Ramsey himself.

Chapter 11

Rod and I had spent a relaxing afternoon skiing, swimming, and soaking in the rays. But the thought of The House, and what we'd found in it, never left me. I knew what had to be done.

I had to go back.

I've always had an inquisitive nature. It was encouraged by my father, who thought people asked too few questions rather than too many.

"Damn the fool," he said, "who came up with the ridiculous adage 'Curiosity killed the cat.' Probably some philandering oaf who didn't want people prying into his business. Curiosity never killed anything. It brings things to life."

He was full of bits of wisdom like that.

"Never apologize for wondering," he said. "It's natural to want to know more."

So why hadn't I asked him more that night, when I had found him sitting in the den with a closed book on his lap, staring blankly at the rug?

"Why aren't you reading?" I asked.

He gave me a rueful smile and said, "I'm afraid I've lost interest."

It was chilling, the way he said it, and I suspected something was wrong. But I didn't ask; I didn't press it. It was the last time I saw him alive.

I was going back to The House, as many times as it took, until I had an answer. Something was going on over there; something was weird, and it wasn't me.

"This is boring, Crane," Rod said. "There's nothing to find out over there."

"I'm not asking you to go with me."

"That's not the point. Just kick back and have a good time. Drink some brewskis, play poker, like we always do. I'm leaving tomorrow, you know."

"I know. But this is important."

He shook his head at me but didn't argue anymore.

I left Rod in the trailer and rowed across the cove in the fishing boat. This time I planned ahead and brought a flashlight. The night was quiet and serene, a three-quarter moon peering down like a lazy eye. The water sloshed beneath the boat as I rowed. I stared at the Ramseys' house, at its lights, which got smaller and smaller the faster the boat moved. Soon the other shore was as distant as a dream. As I let the boat drift up to the land, I felt exiled and completely alone.

Even though I'd justified all this to my satisfaction back at the trailer, I was now starting to wonder what I was up to. My curiosity about this place was beginning to strike me as a little unbalanced, and unbalanced behavior frightened me more than anything The House had to offer. But maybe that was the whole point. Maybe I was driven to do this so I could prove to Rod and Abby—and possibly myself—that I wasn't crazy.

Nothing was stirring in The House. I sat in the boat and ate an apple. When I finished I tossed the core overboard and lay back. The rocking motion coaxed me to sleep. The next thing I knew I was jerking awake, alarmed by an unfamiliar sound.

It took me a moment to place it. Then I was disappointed by the familiarity of it. It was just a car engine. But as I regained focus, I noticed that the car was pulling right up behind The House. It was a van. The headlights were high, painting the surroundings in an eerie glow, making the trees look like skeletons. Then they clicked off and all was dark again. After a moment a light popped on in the front room.

I crept out of the boat. I didn't think it wise

to turn on the flashlight, so I relied on the moon and the light from The House to lead me safely up the path. When I got close I ducked behind a large flowering shrub. From there I could see pretty well.

The van had pulled up right next to the back door. Two men got out of it. A third came out of the house carrying a crate. He handed it to the two others, who slid it inside the van. I strained to get a good look at the men. Late twenties or thirties, dressed in jeans and T-shirts. One had a beard, one was almost platinum-blond, the third had a receding hairline. If you'd seen them in a coffee shop, you wouldn't have looked twice. All three of them went inside the house and came out again with crates, loaded them in the van, then went back inside for more. They didn't speak, just went about their work.

I crept closer to the front of the house and gazed into the window of the front room. The closet door was open, and the light from it spilled over into the room. I saw the bearded man go to the closet, look into it, then call over his shoulder, "That's it."

He had turned to leave when the phone suddenly rang. I jumped back, making a bit of a thud as I dropped my flashlight. Luckily the sound of the phone seemed to obscure that commotion. I sneaked back to the window as the bearded man picked up the receiver.

"Yeah," he said. His voice was muffled, as if underwater, but I could still hear. "Yeah, we just finished up. I guess that'll be the last batch. . . . Well, we've already cleared two mil. I think it would be wise to stop. . . . I know that, but we can't risk another break-in. . . . Why don't we quit while we're ahead?"

He listened for a moment, then:

"I think it's only fair to tell you, we'd expect a bigger cut for another job. The more we do this, the bigger the stakes become. We're talking at least thirty percent now. . . . Well, you just think about it. You know where to find us."

He got ready to hang up, then reconsidered.

"By the way, somebody's been poking around here. Kitchen window was smashed in. Probably just kids, but it adds to my concern. Understand?"

He hung up then and went to the closet, turning off the light. My view of him disappeared. I had seen all I was going to see.

When I turned to go, my mind was still reeling from the information. I felt around in the darkness for my flashlight. Suddenly I sensed a presence, someone very close to me. I could hear breathing. I froze like a frightened animal, but it was too late. Something cold was pressing against my temple.

A voice said, "Move a muscle and you're dead."

I had never been around guns, but it's amazing how easy it is to recognize one. I could feel the circles of steel pressing against my skin. I could smell the metal. Raising my eyes, I could see the platinum-haired man leaning over me.

"Why don't you take a little ride with us," he said.

"Y-You're making a mistake," I stammered.

"No, sir. You're the one who made a mistake. And now you've got to pay the price."

Behind me I felt the flashlight. I touched it and it rolled into my fingers.

"Can't we talk about this?" I asked.

"We got all night to talk."

I stood slowly. The gun stayed pressed against my temple.

"I was just out for a walk," I said.

"Fine. We'll drive you back to where you live."

I started walking with him.

"What's going on in there? I thought the place was empty."

"That's what you get for thinking."

He took my arm and stepped down off the

porch, waiting for me to follow. For that brief second I was higher than he was, able to gain a little bit of an advantage. With all my might, I brought the flashlight down on his arm. I heard the gun fall. I hit him again across the forehead. Then I started running in the direction of the boat.

As I approached the shore, I noticed the boat wasn't where I'd left it. There was nothing but an empty dock and a half a mile of dark lake. It was then that I remembered I hadn't anchored the boat. I squinted and could see it bobbing out in the middle of the lake, lost and alone, like a stray pet.

Footsteps were following me. I waded out into the water, knee deep. It was cold. My teeth chattered uncontrollably. I have to swim for it, I thought.

I heard a gunshot, a blast followed by a whizzing sound. A bullet skimmed the grass next to me. I dove into the water and swam for my life. I heard the gun go off a couple more times, at least one bullet hitting the water next to me and skipping across it like a stone. I dove underneath the surface and swam there as long as my breath lasted. I came up for another quick one, heard another shot, and dove again. This was how I proceeded until I reached my boat.

Somewhere along the line the shots stopped coming, but I couldn't have said when. I didn't hesitate long enough.

I climbed inside the boat and stayed low as I rowed it. I could see The House getting smaller. There were no lights around it. All was quiet. It could have been any other night on the lake. Any other night, except that, for the second time in a week, I was nearly killed.

Chapter 12

═══ "Where have you been?" Abby asked as I knocked on the screen door, then came in.

She and Zan were playing checkers. The day was overcast and cool. The lake was virtually empty. It was the first time I'd seen Abby in real clothes—jeans and a T-shirt. I wanted to scoop her up in my arms and sweep her away. But I reminded myself I was here on a mission.

"I've been busy," I said.

She seemed to take this answer as a lame excuse and focused on the checkerboard.

"Who's that guy hanging around your dock?" Zan inquired.

"Rod Stone. He's a friend of mine."

"Oh, him. He's in our class, right? He's not hard to look at," she informed me.

"She actually forgot about Eric for a day," Abby said, still not looking at me.

"Why don't you bring him over here?" Zan asked.

"He went back to Flanders this morning. He's got a job there."

"Doing what?"

"He works in a hardware store."

Zan digested this, then shrugged. "He's still cute."

"Is your father here? I need to speak to him," I said.

Zan and Abby both looked at me, surprised.

"Yeah, he's here," Zan said. "But he hates to be disturbed."

"It's important," I said.

"If the dock's coming apart again he'll freak," she said.

"Please ask him if he'll see me."

She nodded and started into the cabin, pausing at the door. "Let me know when your friend comes back."

With that she was gone, and Abby and I were left staring at each other. I moved over to her but didn't sit down.

"I waited for you yesterday," she said. "I thought you'd come by. Everyone else went out in the boat, but I stayed here."

"I'm sorry," I said, sitting beside her. "It was only a day."

"It was a long day," she answered.

I felt sick to see her disappointment, and excited at the same time. She had missed me.

She stared a long time at the checker pieces, finally picking one up and rubbing it against her lips.

"I know you think I'm just amusing myself for the summer, but that's not how I feel."

"How do you feel?"

She looked me squarely in the eye. "I like you a lot."

I reached for her hand. She hesitated, then slid her fingers in between mine.

"We're a mismatch, you know," I said. "Your parents would never approve. I wouldn't pass an interview."

"My parents aren't here," she said.

"But if they were . . . I might be interpreted as the 'bad element.'"

"Is that your excuse? You're concerned about my reputation?"

I stared at her fingers, small and slender next to mine, her nails bleached white by all the water and sun. I raised them to my lips and kissed them.

"You're not just using me, are you?" she asked.

I looked at her, stunned.

"Using you? What on earth for?"

She shrugged. "To improve your social status?"

She observed my stunned expression and said, "You're not the only one who gets to be cynical."

"You can think what you want," I said, abruptly dropping her hand.

"What am I supposed to think? You claim to like me, you drop out of sight, you suddenly reappear. Maybe you've got other motives. Have you ever read *An American Tragedy*?"

I felt dizzy now, my chest tightening with anger. I had, in fact, read that book by Theodore Dreiser, which is all about a poor guy who does terrible things just so he can marry a rich girl and move up in the world. But before I could reply Zan appeared in the doorway.

"Daddy says he can see you for a minute. Here's a tip: he's very busy, so make it quick. Second door to the right."

I turned back to Abby and said to her in a low voice, "You obviously don't understand the first thing about me."

"How could I?" she answered. "You never told me."

I let that one go and walked in to see Clark Ramsey.

I tapped on the door of his office and waited for a reply before I entered.

He was sitting behind a desk, leaning back in a leather swivel chair, his feet propped on top of the desk. All the papers were in neat, symmetrical stacks. Bookshelves lined the room. A small TV sat in the corner. Pictures of Zan and Muriel Ramsey adorned the walls. A large Persian rug was in the middle of the room, a couple of chairs and a couch surrounding it.

"Have a seat," Ramsey said, motioning to one of the chairs. I sat.

He stood and approached me, standing with a glass of what appeared to be Scotch in his hand.

"Something to drink?" he asked.

"No, sir."

He remained standing, sipping from his glass, his eyes landing hard on my face.

"What seems to be the problem?"

"Sir?"

"The dock again? I'd hate to dish out another hundred bucks, though I would if necessary. I trust your judgment."

"It's not the dock."

He wrinkled his eyebrows. "What other business do you and I have to discuss?"

"Well . . ."

"I hope it's not my niece. Her parents have big plans for her."

That stopped me cold. I couldn't even think of a way to reply. Ramsey moved to the couch and sat in the middle of it.

"I know Abby is taken with you. I can see why. You're a nice-looking young man, living a carefree existence at the lake. It's almost like a fantasy, isn't it? You have no cares, no concern. Meanwhile, Abby has all manner of obligations staring her in the face. You're a nice escape from that."

"What obligations?"

"She's a congressman's daughter. She'll marry well. I'm sure they already have their eye on a suitable type. Or they'll let her go to Yale and decide for herself, within certain limits."

"Either way," I said, "she won't end up with someone like me. Is that what you're saying?"

"It is," he replied frankly. "As hard as it may be to accept, as antiquated as it may appear, a family like Abby's has certain, shall we say, standards. Only a certain type will do for her."

"And I'm not that type."

"Not now. Of course, things could conceivably change. That's the great thing about this country. We aren't judged by accents or accoutrements or past history. We are judged on our possibilities. The future is what matters. And if you strive toward a promising one, there is no reason that Abby could not one day see you as a realistic suitor. At the moment, however, you're a bit short of the mark."

"I see," I said through tight lips.

"I'm not saying this to be cruel. I think you are a sensible young man and that you can understand logistics. If you see something you want, you have to work in that direction. At the moment, you have certain obstacles to overcome."

"What do you know about my background?"

"Just what I need to know."

I was trying to formulate a response when he leaned closer to me, clutching his drink in both hands.

"Believe it or not, you and I are not that different. Indeed, I come from humble beginnings myself. My sister and I both managed to keep our heads above water. She married an aspiring politician from a patrician background and stood by him. My sister, like Abby, is beautiful and smart. I married a woman with money and have done everything in my power to keep that fortune intact. None of it has been easy. But I don't give up. And I won't have all that sabotaged by a zealous teen in search of a summer romance."

"That isn't my intention, sir."

He leaned back, scrutinizing me. "Be sure that it isn't."

I could hear a clock ticking somewhere. The lake was whipping up under a summer wind, and I could hear it sloshing against the docks. Clark Ramsey stared at me, waiting for my next move.

"I'm not here about Abby," I said.

"Oh?"

"No, sir. I'm here about you."

He set the glass down and crossed his arms, waiting.

"I've discovered something that I think directly affects you and your business," I said.

"What business is that?"

"Your wine business. Abby told me that someone had broken into your winery a couple of days ago and stole some merchandise. Can you tell me what they stole?"

He shrugged. "A few cases of wine. I'm insured. It won't break me."

"I think I saw them."

"Who?"

"The people who stole your wine."

He picked up his glass again and took a long sip from it, keeping his eyes on me.

"Where?" he finally asked.

"Right across the cove, in Dr. Kaplan's house."

He chuckled, swirling the Scotch around in his glass. "My stolen wine is in his empty place?"

"Yes, sir."

"How do you know?"

"Well, to be honest, I had a feeling something was going on over there. I actually broke in to check it out. I found a closet with about a dozen cases of your wine in it. Last night I went back over and I saw three men loading crates into a van."

He seemed interested at last.

"Did you recognize these men?"

"No, sir. I'd never seen them before. I overheard a phone conversation. One guy said they'd already cleared two mil and they wanted to stop, they couldn't risk another break-in."

Suddenly Ramsey threw back his head and laughed.

"Son, if they stole my entire stock they wouldn't get two million dollars for it."

"I'm just telling you what I heard."

"Go on," he said, rubbing a finger across his lip.

"Well, the guy on the phone agreed to another break-in if they'd up his price. I think you're going to be robbed again soon. That's why I'm here, to warn you."

I stopped talking and he sat there rubbing his ring finger across his lip, taking it all in. I had the feeling he was starting to take me seriously at last.

"Did you call the police?" he asked me.

"No, sir. I felt I should come to you before I told anyone."

He nodded again. "I can't believe any of this. It's not as if my wine has any street value. And why would someone take it to Kaplan's? It makes no sense."

"I know. But something's going on. Someone tried to kill me last night."

His head jerked up. "What?"

"They shot at me, sir."

"But that makes no sense at all!"

"I'm just telling you what happened."

He put the glass down again and cracked his knuckles. He kept his eyes on me, as if waiting to see me break and deny my story.

"I'll look into this. In the meantime, I'd advise you not to tell anyone. I don't want this to turn into some nasty business—fodder for the Flanders gossip mill. You can imagine what that kind of story would do to my business. It's all so unpredictable, the way people talk."

"I won't make a move," I said, "until you tell me what to do."

"Good man. I appreciate you telling me. I'm sure there's some explanation. I'll make some calls right now and try to straighten this out."

"Okay. I'll just wait to hear from you."

He stood and offered his hand to me.

"I think I misjudged you, Tyler. You have a strong sense of justice, don't you?"

"I don't know," I answered. "I do know I'm curious."

"Nothing wrong with that," he said, much as my father would have. When we shook hands he smiled at me, and I felt I'd found an ally in a most unlikely person.

As I opened the door to his study I heard him say behind me, "I hope you understood my remarks about Abby. I didn't mean them as an insult. I can understand how you'd be taken with her. She's a remarkable girl."

"I know," I said, and left.

Chapter 13

That night it rained, and the next morning I had plenty of dock work. I got three or four calls before breakfast, and I spent the whole day out in the sunshine, hammering and sawing, envying the people who whipped past me on skis or sailboats. I only took a break to eat a sandwich about four o'clock, then I finally finished up as the sun was going down. I came back to the trailer feeling rich and exhausted.

All I wanted to do was climb into a bathtub with a beer, but as I approached the trailer I saw it wasn't going to be that simple. Someone was sitting on the front step.

It was Abby. She was making a clover chain which was already about three feet long.

"How long have you been here?" I asked.

She shrugged, still working on her chain. "Since lunchtime."

"Just waiting for me?"

"No, I've done other things, too." She

looked up at me with her cool, gray eyes. "I walked down to the dock and back at least six times. I made five clover chains. I found a salamander, but I let him go."

"I've been out working," I said. "With all the rain, there are plenty of docks to put back together."

"I figured that much."

"You waited anyway."

"I waited anyway."

"Want to come inside?"

She stood and let the clover chain drop to her feet. She had yet to smile at me.

"I want to know what's wrong with you," she said.

"Then you better come inside. This might take a while." I attempted a laugh, but she didn't respond.

She began to walk toward the woods. I followed her.

"I don't know how to answer that question," I said.

"Why are you obsessed with the house across the cove?"

"Who told you I was?"

"Uncle Clark. He said you'd broken in there."

"So much for confidence," I mumbled.

"He says you're fixating on that place because of certain problems that you have."

I grabbed her arm. She stopped abruptly, as if she'd been expecting it, and stared me squarely in the eye.

"What problems?" I demanded.

She pried her arm away but continued to stare at me.

"I know about your father. I know he didn't die of heart failure."

I swallowed hard, and felt a cold sweat breaking out across my forehead.

"He did technically. That's what everyone dies of technically," I managed.

"He committed suicide."

I stood there for what seemed like a long time. I tried to focus on the sounds of the birds chirping and the leaves rustling overhead, and the crickets and frogs talking back and forth, trying to lose myself in another language, one where the word I had just heard didn't exist.

It was the first time anyone had ever said the word out loud.

"So what?" I finally said.

"So it's important. You should have told me."

"Why? What does it have to do with you?"

"It helps me understand you."

"Oh, I see. Now you think I'm mentally unstable. I'm having a little bit of a breakdown, like my father. I'm going off the deep end, is that it?"

"No . . ."

"I think it is, Abby. Poor old Tyler, crazy as a bat, just like his old man. He sees things that aren't there. People like that, the underclass, they walk a fine line. They could snap at any minute, those lowlife types. And, after all, his old man offed himself, and you gotta be crazy to do that, and everybody knows it's hereditary!"

I felt a sting across the face, and it took me a second to realize that Abby had slapped me. Her eyes were hot with anger.

"You have no right to talk to me that way!" she shouted.

"Why not?"

"Because I love you, you creep."

I grabbed her, and she let me. I cried against her shoulder, and she let me do that, too.

"He had no right to do it!" I said. "He had no right!"

"No, he didn't."

"I hate him for it."

"That's okay."

"I'll always hate him."

"I don't think you will."

I started to protest, but I couldn't. Because suddenly I was already starting to let go of some of the hate, now that I had said it out loud, now that I had given myself permission to feel it.

≈

We walked down to the dock together, hand in hand. The moon was steadily decreasing in size, now cut in half, as if someone had sliced it neatly down the middle. The water was darker as a result, and everything on the other shore seemed distant.

As we sat with our bare feet dangling in the water, Abby said, "Tell me about it."

"It started with the dog," I said slowly. "His name was Sport. Actually, it was Old Sport, from *The Great Gatsby*. My father was very literary. It was his dog."

Abby nodded, staring at the middle distance.

"My father loved that dog. Talked to him all the time. But that night, he wasn't paying any attention to Sport. Sport wanted to go out for a walk, but Dad didn't take him. He went into his study and I came in later and found him with a book closed on his lap. My father loved to read. And when I asked him why he wasn't reading, he said he'd lost interest. See, I should have known that was a problem. It was the way he said it—he'd lost interest in general."

"Hopelessness," Abby said gently.

"I guess. He was always on the edge of it. He'd disappointed himself in life. He hated his job. My mother was always . . . difficult. He'd struggled and had a lot of disappointments. He took them all personally."

She nodded, pressing my hand against her lips.

"Anyway, that night before I went to bed, Sport was missing. I went through the house calling him. I heard this sound coming from the garage, this kind of humming. It was the radio. I thought, why is someone listening to the radio in the garage? I touched the door and it was warm. I knew right away.

"But I opened it, and the car was running, and there was Sport. He was just this lifeless thing, lying on the cement floor. He was waiting for my father."

I took a deep breath; somehow that was always the hardest part, Sport waiting for my father, waiting until death for him, man's best friend. Maybe that's what I hated my father for the most: betraying everyone's trust, even the dog's.

"I opened the car door. My father was an

ashy color. I didn't touch him or anything. I knew. I just turned off the car and somehow walked back in the house."

Abby squeezed my hand and studied my face, waiting for me to continue.

"What?" she asked, as if reading my mind.

"He was listening to a baseball game on the radio."

She shook her head slightly.

"I don't get it."

"Neither do I," I said. "He hated sports. He told me not to get involved with them. He read and listened to music and studied the stars and plants and birds. He said broadening the mind was the whole point, the whole task of life."

"I guess that was his way of abandoning the task," she said.

"So his whole life was a lie."

She shook her head. "Not his whole life. Just the end. Just that moment. Maybe."

I thought about that for a second before my mind jumped ahead. I rubbed my temples, trying to make it go away. The hurt was too big. I was heading into dangerous waters.

"What?" She nudged me gently.

"My mother."

"What about her?"

"I blame her."

"Why?"

"Because." I swallowed hard. "She pushed him so hard. She was never happy. He knew she was disappointed in him."

"How do you know?"

"You could see it in her face. One time he said to me, 'Your mother looks at me like she wishes she could take me back to the store and get a refund.'"

Abby didn't laugh. But what she said next surprised me.

"He shouldn't have said that to you."

I looked at her.

"Why not?"

"Because he was asking you to take sides."

"You don't understand. You don't know what she's like."

She shook her head slowly. "No, I don't. But I've always heard it takes two people to make a marriage go wrong. And nobody takes his own life because of the way another person looked at him."

I shook my head. I wasn't sure she was capable of understanding. "There's another thing."

"What?" she asked, squeezing my hand.

"My father believed in me. He thought I was going places. That should have been enough to keep him going, right? But he decided not to stick around for it. So I have to figure he lost faith. In me, Abby. He lost faith in me. And it's her fault."

"But how?"

"Because *she* didn't believe in me. She thought I was just like him, destined to repeat his mistakes. Whenever I'd bring home a bad grade? She'd just look at him with this weird smile on her face. She wanted to prove him wrong. And I can't help thinking she succeeded."

"No mother would do that."

"Mine would."

I saw her staring at me, searching my face and wanting to understand. I shook my head, fighting back a tightness in my throat.

"Oh, Abby, don't you get it? If he didn't believe in me, who's going to?"

She took my face in her hands and looked right at me with those eyes, the strength and color of iron.

"I'm going to," she said. "And so are you. You, Tyler Crane, are going to believe in yourself. You're going to believe you're important, because you are."

I kissed her gratefully, then held her as tight as I could. I let myself trust her. It was an enormous, scary feeling, like getting sucked into the dam.

"I'm glad you told me," she said.

"I'm glad you made me."

It was late when I walked her back. I didn't go all the way, just a few steps past Tom Wheat's place. I remembered Clark Ramsey's words about my future with Abby, but I tried to push them from my mind.

"Come by and see me tomorrow," Abby said.

"I will."

"Promise?"

"Abby, you know your uncle gave me a warning. Your family doesn't want us together."

"I don't care."

"What about all those plans your parents have for you, and those guys at Yale you're going to marry?"

She laughed. "I love my parents, Tyler, but honestly, I've got my *own* plans."

"I love you," I said.

She smiled. "It took you long enough to figure it out."

I kissed her there, in plain view, under the haze of the half-moon. It was the kind of moment that never leaves. The kind that gets you through a long night.

Then I turned and went back to the trailer, feeling light and happy.

I was whistling an old Beatles song as I opened the door. I was thinking about grabbing a beer and getting in the bath. I tried to turn on a light, but nothing happened. Then I heard a sound that you only have to hear once to understand.

It was the sound of a revolver being cocked.

"So this is how the other side lives," said a voice in the darkness.

I stood still, surprised by my fate.

Abby

Chapter 14

"Men are like bonds," Zan said, rubbing orange-colored suntan goop on her legs. "They're really worthless until they mature."

She laughed and waited for me to do the same. She was trying to cheer me up.

"Who told you that?"

"It's something Mom says."

"I don't like any sentence that starts 'Men are like . . .' or 'Women are like. . . .' It's always some stupid generalization."

"Generalizations are useful. People like the idea of truth condensed. That's what Daddy says."

"Maybe you shouldn't listen to your parents so much."

"Oh, like you don't listen to yours? Like you're this rebellious character? When have you ever even talked back to your parents?"

"This year," I said defensively. "My mother wanted me to be on the debate team because that was what she did in high school. I finally said, 'Mom, who wants to make a hobby out of arguing?' "

Zan giggled. She loved to hear about disruptions in my house; it seemed to make her feel less alone.

"What did she say?" Zan asked.

"Nothing. But my dad said, 'Your mother, that's who. She's turned arguing into an art form.' "

Zan's eyes glowed. "Then what happened? Did they fight?"

I shrugged. "A little."

I didn't want to tell her that my mother only giggled and my father tickled her and made her laugh harder. That stuff seemed silly to me, but I knew it would make Zan feel insecure. Her parents never joked around.

She finished oiling herself and lay back like a human sacrifice to the sun. I stared at her, feeling aggravated. I always got this way around Zan after a week. She was my cousin and I loved her in that family sense. We even had fun together occasionally. But she wore on my nerves after a while, especially if something was bugging me. And this day, something was definitely bugging me.

"You are in a pique, aren't you?" she asked.

"I don't even know what a pique is."

"A snit, basically. But don't you love that word? Mommy uses it. She says once you hit a certain tax bracket, you get in piques, not snits. You experience ennui, not boredom. You have altercations, not squabbles. She's got a whole list of them."

"Good for Aunt Muriel. She's an encyclopedia of insults."

"Honestly, Abby. You're so grumpy."

"Don't you mean irascible?"

She giggled. "I'm not even going to let you get to me today. I'm too happy."

Eric had called her twice in one day, and had wired a half dozen long-stem red roses to the house. I hated to admit it, but her happiness was only adding to my frustration.

"I just don't understand it," I said, peeling a thin layer of skin off my arm. It was coming off in sheets now. I felt like a snake, molting.

"That's what I was trying to tell you about men. You can't expect too much from them until they grow up."

"But Tyler's different. He wouldn't say he was coming if he didn't mean it."

"Maybe something else came up."

"That was days ago. He couldn't even call?"

"If it's worrying you so much, go over there."

"I did. It looks like . . ." I stopped myself from saying it, partly because I didn't want to believe it, and partly because I didn't want to do anything to help prove Zan's theory about men.

But she got it anyway. "Like he just picked up and left?"

"He wouldn't have done that."

Zan rolled over on her side and planted a world-weary stare on me.

"Let it go, Abby. We've got a week of vacation left and I don't want you ruining it by moping over some guy."

"First of all, look who's talking. Your whole world revolves around Eric's phone calls."

"But that's different. This is some guy you hardly know. Some guy who fixed our dock."

"What the hell does that mean? You met him. You know he's not just 'some guy.' "

"I know he's *different*," she said, as if the word implied a host of unpleasant things.

"What's wrong with different? You're different."

Zan looked hurt, and I felt bad right away. She was family, after all. I'd spent vacations with her for as long as I could remember. She was an only child who seemed to think of me as a sister.

She wrote me long letters on pretty stationery that smelled like perfume. She wrote about what she bought, who she saw at school, who asked her out. Actually, she always sounded lonely in her letters, and I always felt obligated to do something about it. I wasn't lonely; I had two younger sisters and usually a houseful of people. My parents got along with each other.

"Your cousin doesn't have the easiest life," my mother was always explaining to me. "Clark spends too much time working. Muriel isn't easy. Zan needs someone like you to talk to."

I tried to be that person, but at the moment I desperately needed someone to listen to *me*.

I was fifteen years old and had never had a boyfriend.

This was something a lot of people—other girls my age especially—found amazing about me. From the time the girls I knew turned twelve, it was like a race to get a boyfriend, to write some guy's name on a book cover, to get and give wildly expensive presents at Christmas and on Valentine's Day, to talk on the phone and pick out an "our song" and then cry whenever it came on the radio. But this getting and maintaining of a boyfriend did not interest me.

Sometimes people assumed this was a result of my being the daughter of a politician. But the truth was, in northern Virginia there were lots of girls with politicians for fathers, some of them much bigger deals than mine. They had boyfriends. The truth was something a lot simpler, and not very amazing at all: I had never met a guy who made me want to deface school property.

Tyler was different—in every way, he was different. Now that I'd met Tyler, I could finally see what all the fuss was about. It first hit me when I saw him standing on the dock with his shirt off, and his face all red from the sun, hammering nails into planks. When he looked at me with those dark, worried eyes, I thought, I could write this guy's name on the cover of my physical science textbook. I could spray-paint a bathroom wall. I could carve our initials in a tree. Tyler Crane and me, forever.

Daddy once said, "As soon as Abby finds out a guy is flesh and blood, she loses interest."

This was after I had begged him to fix me up with the son of a fellow congressman, who looked so good in his school pictures, then immediately disappointed me on a date.

"You've got to let people have flaws," he told me. "Otherwise you'll be miserable."

"Don't lecture her, Donald," Mom had said.

"As soon as she can embrace someone's flaws, she'll know she's in love."

What my parents didn't understand was that it wasn't the presence of flaws that I found disappointing in people; it was the absence of them. All the guys I knew were so boring. Their lives were organized, structured. They all wore the right clothes, had the right cars, got the right grades, and were going to the right colleges. They could see their lives mapped out ahead of them, and nothing was going to stop them from reaching their goals. Like the son of this congressman. He knew what college he'd go to, what law school, what kind of law he'd practice, and even what county he'd practice in—and he'd only just gotten his driver's license.

These guys didn't leave any room for chance. They had ambition, but absolutely no daring. Tyler had a lot of daring. Considering all he'd been through, it seemed like a courageous act for him just to get out of bed in the morning. I had a sense that life with Tyler would always be an adventure. But now it seemed the adventure was over before it could begin.

"Zan, sweetie! Eric's on the phone!" Aunt Muriel called out to us. She was always happy when Eric called. He was the son of a judge, a suitable match for Zan.

Zan got to her feet, smiling sympathetically at me.

"You'll be all right while I'm gone, won't you? You won't try to kill yourself or anything?"

"Zan!"

"It's just a joke," she said innocently, then shook her head and ran off.

I sat on the dock staring out at the water, waiting to see Tyler go by. I almost didn't want to. I simply wouldn't accept that he was somewhere on the lake, free to move about as he chose, avoiding me. He said he loved me. It takes a cold heart to lie about something like that. And whatever his shortcomings were, a cold heart wasn't one of them.

So where was he?

I knew what Zan would say—that it was impossible to rely on "people like that." They never kept their word, they moved on when they felt like it, they didn't understand obligations, "those people."

Zan and I were privileged, as they say. But I didn't feel that Zan and I were that much alike. She took herself seriously, and paid way too much attention to appearance, to clothes and to money. She was a terrible snob.

I hoped I wasn't that way. I tried not to judge people the way Zan did. My parents were always lecturing me about cross sections. They wanted me to experience cross sections; they wanted me to know that not everyone had the things I had, and that money wasn't what made a person exceptional.

Daddy was fond of quoting to me from the first chapter of *The Great Gatsby,* that part where Nick's father says whenever you feel tempted to judge people, remember that not everyone has had the advantages you've had. This, he said, ought to be the real Golden Rule. Imagine my surprise when Tyler said his father named their dog Old Sport, straight from *Gatsby.* If I didn't already know we were meant for each other, I knew it then.

I'd never met anyone like Tyler. I'd never seen a guy my age hammering planks together. It was really attractive to me, the idea of a guy doing something with his hands so he could earn a living. The guys I knew only used their hands to wash their BMWs on weekends. But this part was only the beginning of the attraction. It grew from there. After fifteen years, I had finally found a guy I was willing to trust enough to say "I love you" to.

And then he was gone.

I stared at the house across the cove. It looked like something out of a novel, with its bay windows and balconies, the grass that had grown up around the lot, the weeds overrunning the dock. Suddenly I felt a sort of calling to it, like he did, but I knew it was only because it reminded me of Tyler. It was my only other connection to him besides the empty trailer and the path that led between our place and his.

In the middle was the cabin of that guy we had talked to that day, Tom, who was trying to write a novel. I saw him on the deck some days, typing and drinking, dozing in the sun. Tyler seemed to like him. They were friends.

They were friends.

I stared at the cabin with a surge of hope. He might know something. It was worth a try.

"Eric's a doll," Zan said as she came back to the dock. "He wants me to marry him in 1999. Can you believe it? He's picked the year."

She sat down beside me and studied my expression.

"Bad news, Abby," she said in a low voice. "Eric says Tyler Crane is kind of . . . a loser. He knows him from school."

" 'A loser'?"

She shrugged. "Yeah."

"What's his definition of a loser? Somebody who keeps breaking up and getting back together with the same person, maybe?"

Zan gave me a disappointed look.

"Abby, you think you want love. But you don't even understand what it is."

She lay down on her towel, facing the sun, feeling secure in her understanding of love. She thought it was something that kept you guessing. But I knew better. And so did Tyler.

Wherever he was.

Chapter 15

〰 My cousin Zan is what you call a Superlative, with those stunning features, chiseled cheekbones, jet-black hair, and sky-blue eyes. Compared with that, everything about me is watered down. My face is perfectly round, with no definition to it. My eyes are gray, struggling to be blue but never quite getting there. I keep my hair short, like a boy's, which is really not in fashion. But I always have the feeling that cutting my hair short makes me look brave. It's putting my face out there to confront the world. It says, "Here I am. You got a problem with it?"

Tyler didn't have a problem with it. He loved it without ever saying so, without ever paying me one of those drippy compliments that you never believe. Tyler could talk with his face. He wore his thoughts there. And when I watched his face, I figured out that love wasn't just how you felt about another person; it was also about how that person made you feel about yourself. Tyler made me feel like a Superlative. Or maybe that not being a Superlative wasn't important.

At night I lay awake and wondered about him, trying to picture him packing his things up and going back to town, never worrying about telling me goodbye. Even if an emergency had come up, he would have told me. He would have given me his phone number. Tyler wasn't a deserter. That was the thing he hated his father for —skipping out on him. He wouldn't do it to me.

The third morning after he was missing, Aunt Muriel and Uncle Clark decided to take the boat out. Uncle Clark was in a good mood. Zan was thrilled at having another chance to water-ski, but I couldn't get into the spirit of it. I only had six days left to find Tyler. I could almost hear a clock ticking in my head.

"I think I'll just stay here and sunbathe," I told them.

"You've had enough sun already," Uncle Clark said. "You're peeling all over. Your parents will kill me if I send you home with sun poisoning."

"I'll wear sunscreen."

"Then what's the point of sunbathing?" Uncle Clark seemed anxious for me to come along.

Zan gave me a hard look, but had given up on me in general.

"Let her be, Clark," Aunt Muriel said. "It's her vacation; let her do what she wants."

He gave in at last, and I sat on the dock and watched the boat move out into the water. I sat there for a while, listening to the radio, until the boat took a turn and disappeared around the corner of the cove. Then I slipped on my shorts and a T-shirt and headed to the cabin next door.

Tom Wheat looked pleased to see me, even though I wasn't convinced he knew who I was. He served me up a glass of orange juice and seated me out on the balcony, chattering away about his work. His eyes were bleary, and he kept adding champagne to his own orange juice, while trying to do the same to mine.

"No thank you," I insisted. "I'm not much of a drinker."

"Good for you," he said, beaming.

I smiled back at him.

"How's your novel going?" I asked.

"It's going to be the death of me, that's how it's going. Take my advice, never aspire to write a word."

"What's it about?"

"It's about a man who thinks he's a writer

until, one very sad summer, he realizes that he's only a man who dreams and drinks too much."

He took a swig of his drink and gazed out at the lake.

"Do you know who I am?" I asked.

"No. And I don't care. You're lovely to look at, and I sense you are someone very nice."

"I met you once with Tyler."

"Ah, Tyler Crane. It's coming back to me now. You were frolicking with him neath the canopy of the oaks and pines. Where is our young friend? I miss his company."

"So do I."

He looked surprised, then smiled. "Surely we miss him differently."

"Surely," I agreed.

"Has all gone sour?"

"I don't know."

"Well," he sighed, deep and low, "as our friend Will Shakespeare said, 'Men have died from time to time, and worms have eaten them, but not for love.' I suppose that applies to the fairer sex as well."

"I don't believe he'd do anything to hurt me," I declared.

"Nor do I," he boomed, slamming his glass down. "He really is a fine specimen, our Tyler

Crane. Honestly, he has saved me from myself more times than you know."

He leaned across the table, and I was aware of leaning away from him.

"I always got the feeling he liked me. He listens. He asks questions and seems to yearn for the answers. I love him as a son. Or I suppose I do. Since I don't have sons it's hard to say."

"Do you know what's happened to him?"

His eyes widened and he jutted his bottom lip out.

"No. Do you?"

"No. That's why I'm here."

Tom Wheat poured another dose of champagne into his orange juice.

"Has he disappeared?" he asked.

"I think so."

He rested his chin against his fist and seemed to be thinking deeply. After a moment I realized he was about to doze off.

"Mr. Wheat?"

"Yes, darling," he said, snapping to.

"I'm worried about him."

"You're right to worry."

"Do you have any idea what could have happened to him?"

He shook his head slowly. "I wish I could help."

I took a sip of orange juice, trying to think of how to proceed.

"You know," I offered, "he was concerned about that house across the cove. The Kaplan house. He thought something strange was going on over there."

"Did he really?"

"He thought someone was after him."

"*He* should have been the novelist."

"Can you please help me?" I was aware of how desperate I sounded, and it wasn't nearly as desperate as I felt. This guy was basically a pathetic drunk, and he was my only hope.

"What can I do?"

"I don't know."

I pounded my fist on my thigh out of frustration. Without even realizing it I started to cry. Tom Wheat noticed and handed me a handkerchief.

"Tell me what to do," he said, leaning over me, swiping at my cheeks. "I'll help as much as I can."

"I don't know."

He put his hand on my arm. "You love Tyler, don't you."

I felt strong all of a sudden, just hearing the sound of that. I was unaccustomed to adults talking to me that way, acknowledging that I could have the same feelings they had.

"Yes. Very much," I said.

"I envy you. It's a wonderful, terrible feeling."

"Maybe we can go over to that house," I said. "Just to have a look around."

"Anytime. Just let me know."

I nodded and stood up. I could see my uncle's boat far off up the lake, heading in our direction.

"Tell me something," Tom said, eyeing me steadily, suddenly very sober. "You're not cut from the same cloth, are you."

"What?"

"You're from a more expensive bolt, aren't you."

"I guess. But that doesn't matter."

"No, it shouldn't, yet so often it does. Those details shouldn't complicate matters. God knows —and if He doesn't, somebody ought to inform Him—things are hard enough down here as it is."

"You know about Tyler's father, don't you?" I asked.

Tom Wheat drew a blank stare, then something seemed to kick in.

"He died recently."

"He killed himself," I said.

"Oh, Mother Mary," he replied, sinking into his chair. "Life is full of horror. Why do we greet each day with hope? What purpose is there in it?"

"I'll come back soon," I said as I started toward the door.

His voice stopped me.

"Tyler wouldn't have done that, would he?"

I turned to him slowly. I couldn't pretend the thought had never occurred to me. But I wouldn't believe it.

"No," I said firmly. "He hated his father for it."

"Hate makes us strangers to ourselves," Tom said.

Chapter 16

The next morning I got up early, while everyone was still sleeping, and went over to Tyler's trailer. It was the third time I'd gone there, feeling all giddy with hope, just to be disappointed by the same hollow sound each time I knocked on the door. I knew he wasn't there, but I was looking for any connection to him. Any reason to believe he hadn't disappeared into thin air.

I circled the trailer, then sat on the step, pretending I was waiting for him to come home from work. Possibly an hour passed before a thought occurred to me like a bolt from the blue: to get inside, to see what he left behind.

I was prepared to break a window, but first I tried the doorknob on the off chance it was unlocked. To my surprise, it turned easily and swung open. How could this be? Tyler was always so careful about locking the door, even when he just walked down to the dock. Because the place didn't belong to him, he was especially careful about taking care of it.

The inside of the trailer looked pretty much the same as always. Nothing was out of place. I guess I was thinking it would look all ransacked, the way places do in the movies when someone from the underworld has paid a visit. But the neatness of the trailer spooked me just as much. There was usually something out of place when Tyler was around. A beer can here, a dirty plate there, the wadded-up pages of a newspaper. Now, nothing. Not even a pair of shoes.

I went to the kitchen and opened the fridge. It was empty except for two cans of beer. There was no food in the cabinets either. The sink was scrubbed, and there were clean dishes in the drying rack.

I found the bathroom in the same pristine state. No toothbrush, no soap, no shampoo. The towels weren't damp. The shower was bone-dry.

Finally, I made my way into the bedroom. This was the hardest part. I'd never been in it, but somehow it was where I felt the closest to Tyler. I pictured him sleeping on the small double bed, tossing and turning under the candlewick bedspread, or lying still and awake, thinking of his father. Did he dream about finding him? Did he wake up and cry out?

Did he ever think of me?

I sat on the bed and fingered the fringe on the bedspread, annoyed with myself for having such a selfish thought. On the scale of things worth lying awake about in Tyler's life, I had to be way down there. But suddenly it was important for me to believe that he'd at least spent a moment or two remembering my face, or things we said to each other. It was important because, as I looked around, I realized that what I'd feared was true—he had just picked up and left.

Sitting there, I allowed myself to fall into some kind of trance. I pictured Tyler and myself living there, a married couple. It was such a ridiculously small and shabby place, yet I knew that plenty of people called a place like this home. I remembered a much older girl in my town who had gotten pregnant in her senior year in high school, married the father, and ended up living in "a mobile home," so people whispered darkly, as if she'd ended up living in a dungeon. That image always filled me with dread, but I was surprised to find myself not at all depressed by the idea of living here with Tyler. These were the crazy things love did to you, I thought. They made you willing to live in small, shabby spaces. Happiness could make everything different. Because when I was alone here with Tyler, the distance between us and the walls didn't matter a bit.

On a whim, I lifted up the spread and checked under the bed. It was something I always did in strange rooms, hotel rooms, places that seemed to suck your belongings into a vacuum. At first I didn't see anything. Then I noticed a dark lump, way back in the left corner. I reached in and felt something like canvas. I pulled hard and a backpack came out, plain, fatigue-colored, with the initials TC written in one corner in black Magic Marker.

I unzipped it eagerly, and Tyler's things spilled out. Shirts, shorts, jeans, socks. I put one of his T-shirts against my face. It smelled the way he did—a combination of fresh air, trees, lake water, and aloe lotion.

I cried into his T-shirt for one pathetic moment before my brain kicked into action.

Why? Why would he leave his clothes behind?

The only possible answers had to be taken seriously. He was in a hurry, on the run, afraid. Of whom? Why? Or he didn't leave by choice. He was forced to leave.

And no one had found the backpack.

Suddenly I felt afraid, and I began to shove the clothes into the pack. I had to get out. I wasn't safe. Neither was Tyler, wherever he was —if it wasn't too late.

As I was stuffing clothes into the pack, my knuckles hit something hard and cold. I pushed my hand deeper into the bag and found a bottle. I pulled it out and stared at it for what seemed like a long time. It was a bottle of Uncle Clark's wine.

What was it doing here? Tyler wouldn't steal a bottle of wine. Uncle Clark had a couple of cases in the house, and he was only too happy to give it away to anyone who asked. Maybe Uncle Clark did give it to him, and Tyler was saving it for some special occasion. Or for some kind of memento. But why did he hide it? And, again, why would he leave it behind?

I stuffed the wine in the backpack, tucked it under my arm, and made my way out of the trailer, taking a careful look all around. I had the feeling I was being watched, even though I knew I was just being paranoid. Everything about this discovery had left me feeling unsettled.

The sun was blazing down from the east corner of the sky now. It was probably ten o'clock, and everybody would wonder where I was. I was trying to think of a place to hide the knapsack when a sudden voice made me jump.

"Top of the morning to you!"

It was Tom Wheat, waving to me from his deck.

"What does that saying mean, anyway?" he boomed. "A morning doesn't have a top, and if it did, why would anyone want to possess it? Or bestow it? Leave it to the Irish to come up with a nonsensical greeting."

"Shhh!" I said, holding my finger to my lips.

"Shhh? Are we being observed by enemy forces?"

"Can I come up?" I asked in a hushed tone.

"You may come up, you may stay up, you may break fast with me. I have two small eggs and a lean strip of bacon to share, and I do so willingly, and with great joy . . ."

I let him babble as I made my way up the steps.

"I need a favor," I said breathlessly.

"And I am in need of supplying one. I am bored to distraction with myself and my needs. Name the favor—it will be delivered before sundown."

I thrust the knapsack at him. "You have to hold on to this," I said.

He stood there staring at it, and me, as if wondering what came next. The thing he seemed to regret the most was having to put down his orange juice, which I was sure contained more than just the recommended daily allowance of vitamin C.

"And what is this?" he inquired, taking it, inspecting it, holding it at arm's length.

"It belonged . . . *belongs* to Tyler. I found it in the trailer."

"You still haven't located our friend?"

"No."

"You still believe him to be involved in all manner of subterfuge?"

"I know you don't believe me."

"My dear girl, I believe everything. It is one of my true failings in life. I haven't any capacity for skepticism. Poltergeists, UFOs, positive thinking, spontaneous human combustion. I haven't the heart to doubt any of these things, which is why I can't commit to any sort of religious following. I believe them all! They sound so neat and tidy. Who am I to go poking holes?"

"Mr. Wheat," I said, a bit impatiently, "I'm very worried. I know something has happened to Tyler. His trailer looks like it's been abandoned, but I found this under the bed. He didn't take his clothes. Why would he leave and not take them? It doesn't make sense. Something strange is going on."

"I believe you," he said. "Are you thirsty?"

"No." I put my hand on his arm and

squeezed, for emphasis. "This is very important. I have to trust you."

"Please do. No one has in so long."

"Don't tell anyone."

"On my honor. What there is left of it, anyway."

"Thank you. Now I have to run."

I could see people moving around in our place, breakfast being laid out on the table. If they hadn't missed me already they would soon.

"Oho! What's this?"

Tom had located the bottle of wine, as if by instinct, and was holding it up in the light.

"Put that away! And don't drink it!"

"Have no fear," he said. "Red wine and I parted company years ago."

Chapter 17

"Zan, you're not listening to me."

"I am so."

"You're filing your nails."

"I can listen *and* file my nails. I'm not that myopic."

She had clearly devoted this summer to improving her vocabulary, even though she frequently put her new words to the wrong use.

"He's in trouble," I said. "And myopic means shortsighted."

"He's gone is what he is. And I know what myopic means."

"I found his clothes there."

"Maybe he didn't like them. Or just forgot about them. I wish you wouldn't make a federal case out of this. I'm depressed enough about the weather."

It had turned gray again, a monster of a cloud hanging low over the horizon. It looked like a summer storm would be on us any moment.

Zan and I were playing cards on the porch. Music came through in weak spurts on the radio, interrupted by bursts of static. That was always an indication of bad weather to come.

"Daddy is so insane," she said, "taking the boat out on a day like this. And I don't know why Mommy went with him. She usually resists his stupid ideas."

I didn't say anything to that. Zan put her nail file down and stared at me. I could feel that she wanted to bring up a difficult subject, but I resisted giving her the opening. Unfortunately, with Zan, my resistance didn't count for much.

"Abby, be realistic," she said. "It's not like you were going to marry the guy."

I looked at her. It would have been so easy to agree and let it go at that.

"Why not?" I challenged.

She rolled her eyes.

"Why not, Zan? Because I'm too young? You and Eric have picked the year already."

"I know, but . . ."

I waited, aware that even Zan didn't have the gall to finish the sentence.

"What?" I said. "Tyler is not 'our kind of people'?"

She shrugged. "You said it, not me."

"That's ridiculous. What century is this? News flash, Zan: the concept of arranged marriages is out."

"Is it?" she asked coyly, tossing her thick dark hair over her shoulder.

"Well, ask yourself. What if Eric didn't have any money? What if his father was a mechanic instead of a judge?"

"That's not the case," she said evasively, inspecting her nails.

"People marry for love these days, if you hadn't noticed."

A little sound came from her throat. "Mommy says it's just as easy to love a man with money."

"Well, I think that's pathetic."

"Really? Are you prepared to go to work to support him? It's one thing to go to college and have a career because you want to. It's another to go through all that just to pay the bills."

"Why should the man be the breadwinner? And anyway, Tyler can be anything he wants to be. That's what's so great about America. Anybody can make it."

"You really believe that stuff?"

"Of course I do. It was the whole point of my father's campaign."

She nodded knowingly. "And your father has you in a private school. Why? If he thought the masses were so great, wouldn't he have you mixing with them?"

I looked away from her. I didn't want to answer that question, mainly because it touched a sore spot. I could have told her what my parents said—that the public schools in our area weren't up to snuff (thanks to spending cuts by the *other* party), and they had my future to think of. But it was an inconsistency that bothered me.

"Zan," I said, eager to change the subject. "You've got to help me find Tyler."

"Why? And how? I hardly know the guy."

"You know his friend, don't you? Rod Stone?"

"I know who he is. I saw him around at school. But he never looked as good as he did on the dock that day. Still, if it weren't for Eric, I'd probably be tempted to do some serious investigating when school starts."

"You don't know his phone number, do you?"

"Of course not."

"Or his father's name?"

She hesitated, making a perfect oval out of the nail on her ring finger, sculpting it like a piece of marble.

"His father owns some car dealership."

"Do you know what it's called?"

She shrugged, sighing impatiently.

"Stone something. Cadillac. Something with a C."

"Thanks," I said, rushing inside the cabin for the kitchen phone.

"You're not calling long-distance, are you?" Zan asked. "Daddy hates that."

I called directory assistance, asking for Stone Cadillac in Flanders.

"I have no listing for Stone Cadillac," said the operator in an annoying, whiny tone.

"Stone something. It starts with C."

There was a long pause.

"Stone Chrysler?" she finally said.

"That must be it."

"Hold for the number."

≡

A harried voice answered.

"Is Rod Stone there?" I asked.

"No, he doesn't work here. This is his father's business."

"I'm trying to find Rod. Can you help me?"

A pause. Then, "Mr. Stone doesn't like us to give out his home number."

"Couldn't you make an exception? It's very important."

"No, ma'am. It's policy."

I sat there chewing my nail to the quick, trying to think of another approach, when the voice came back.

"Have you tried the hardware store?"

"What hardware store?"

"Where Rod works. Castle Hardware. He's probably there now."

I called information again.

"Abby, come on, I'm bored!" Zan called out. "Come play cards with me!"

"Castle Hardware, can I help you?"

"Yes, is Rod Stone there?"

"You got him."

"Hi. You don't know me. I'm a friend of Tyler Crane's."

There was a long pause.

"Hello?"

"I'm listening."

"I think something's happened to him."

"Jeff, turn down the radio!" he yelled.

"What's wrong?" he came back, with a worried voice. "He didn't wreck the boat, did he? He didn't drown or anything?"

"No. He's just . . . well . . . he's disappeared."

Another pause.

"Who is this?" he asked.

"Abby Winston. I'm staying with the Ramseys."

"Oh, yeah. He mentioned you. Listen, I wouldn't be too worried about him. Tyler's not the settling-down type. He's kinda restless. I'm sure he'll give you a call sometime."

"You don't understand. I think something has happened to him. He told my uncle that someone tried to shoot at him, over at this house across the cove."

"Oh, hell, he's not still on that kick, is he?"

"I don't know what kick he's on," I said, feeling tearful. "I don't know where he is. No one's in the trailer. It's all deserted except for his clothes. And he wouldn't have left without telling me, I know it."

I was nearly crying now.

"Look, he's been known to do things like this before. He's got a history of running away. I'm not saying he'd bag out on you. But he's got a few things on his mind."

"I know all about his father."

"Then you ought to understand."

"But where would he go? Where does he live?"

Rod hesitated and exhaled again.

"There's nobody at his house. It's on the market right now."

"Where's his mother? Could you give me her number?"

"Look, Abby, I know Tyler likes you, 'cause he told me he did. But there are certain things you shouldn't go sticking your nose into. Take my advice—leave his mother out of this."

"Somebody has to care about Tyler besides me."

"I care."

"Then give me the number."

"All right. It's your funeral."

"I wish you wouldn't use that expression."

"555-0224. That's his aunt's house. His mother'll be there."

"Thanks, Rod."

"Listen. Call me if you find out anything."

I sat there for a few minutes, trying to talk myself out of dialing the number. *Stay out of it,* said a small voice inside me. *You don't know these people. Let it pass, and the summer will end, and you'll be back at school with everything that is familiar.*

The image of that, so dull and predictable, stirred me to act.

I dialed the number and chewed my fingernails as it rang several times. I was about to hang up when someone answered, a woman with a helpless kind of voice.

"May I speak to Mrs. Crane?"

"Who is this?"

"I'm a friend of Tyler's. Is this his aunt?"

"They've gone shopping. I don't know when they'll be back. *We* never go anywhere."

"Excuse me?"

"We used to go places. You don't know how hard it is having no money, never going anywhere. It's my husband's fault."

"Mrs. Crane? Is this Tyler's mother?"

"Tyler was difficult. He was fussy. I practically raised him by myself. His father never showed any interest."

"Mrs. Crane, my name is Abby. I'm a friend of Tyler's. I was wondering if maybe he was with you . . . if you've seen him lately."

"He left me. Everyone leaves me."

"Do you know where he is?"

"He doesn't care what happens to me. He wishes it was me who was dead."

"Mrs. Crane . . ."

"He said so. He told me so."

"Then he's with you?"

"We never go anywhere."

What was wrong with her? Why wasn't she hearing me?

"I'm afraid something has happened to him," I said. "You've got to help me."

"We used to go to movies, at least. Why should I have to live poor? I thought he was going somewhere. I thought he would be a judge."

"Oh my God," I whispered, holding the phone away from my face. "Oh, Tyler."

"I'm sorry I bothered you, Mrs. Crane," I said into the phone.

"I'm just so tired," she said. I hung up before I could hear any more.

Chapter 18

≈ That night it stormed. I lay awake in my sleeping bag on the screened-in porch, where Zan and I always insisted on sleeping, even though there were three empty guest rooms in the house. I liked lying so close to the water and the fresh air, listening to all the night sounds. A storm just added to the mystery of the night, lightning streaking across the sky and thunder rumbling intermittently, like trains crashing through the silence. I could hear the water whipping up, lapping against the dock. I didn't understand how anyone could sleep through such an impressive show of nature, but Zan was out like a light. All was still inside the cabin. I felt like the only living thing in the universe.

Even without the storm, I would have been awake. I was thinking of Tyler, of my conversations with Rod and Tyler's mother and Tom Wheat, going over all the possibilities of his whereabouts. But most of all, I was thinking about what Aunt Muriel had said to me before I went to bed.

She called me into her bedroom about ten o'clock and shut the door carefully behind her. It always made me feel weird to be in there, mainly because it lacked any sign of Uncle Clark. He slept in another room down the hall. Aunt Muriel behaved as if there were nothing out of the ordinary about this. Even during my parents' rockiest moments (particularly right after Daddy got elected to Congress), they always shared a room. They went there to have private conversations, to fight, to do other things that kids my age don't like to think of their parents doing. But that room was what always made me know that my parents were connected, entangled, however messily. Their clothes clumped together on the bed or the chairs; Mom's jewelry lived beside Daddy's cuff links and tie tacks. If I'd ever walked into that room and found it looking the way Aunt Muriel's did—all floral, perfumey, feminine, neat—I'd have felt like my universe was crumbling. Zan and I never talked about this, even though I sometimes sensed she wanted to.

I sat on a love seat nestled inside a bay window and watched Aunt Muriel as she paced noiselessly across the carpet, rubbing her chin, gathering her thoughts. Even in her thick terry-cloth bathrobe, she looked well put together, like she was about to dash out somewhere. She still had on makeup, bracelets, rings, and earrings, and she still smelled like an overproductive flower garden.

"Abby, darling," she finally said. "You know you are my favorite niece. I love you like a daughter."

"Thanks," I said, a little taken aback. Aunt Muriel wasn't the confessional type. She spent most of her time hiding behind women's magazines, doing leg lifts, and telling Zan and me not to stay out in the sun too long.

"That's why I want to take you into my confidence. I want to tell you a story that not many people get to hear. Not even Zan. Especially Zan."

"Okay," I said, swallowing nervously.

"I think you know a little bit about my history before I married. I was raised with money. Those mills come from my side of the family. There has never been a time in my life when I have ever had to worry about an unpaid bill, or even look at the price tag on a dress. You've been raised pretty much the same way. So has Zan."

I wanted to protest here. Even though we were what I guess you'd call wealthy, I still had to look at the price tag on a dress. My folks didn't mind spending, but they insisted on getting their money's worth. But I didn't bring this up. I kept quiet.

"Because I was surrounded by wealth, I never really appreciated the value of it. I even began to resent it. When I was sixteen or seventeen, I went through a rebellious stage. I wanted to prove to my parents that I didn't need money, that there was no difference between rich and poor. I felt that these were false distinctions, and I wanted to renounce them."

She sat in a chair across from me, twisting the rings around on her fingers.

"So you can imagine what I did. I started dating every fellow I could find from the wrong side of the tracks. I wasn't picky. I was partial to good looks, but the only other qualification was that they didn't have two cents to rub together."

I tensed up. I was starting to sense where this was heading, and I didn't like it. Still, I kept quiet.

"Then one day I met this particular young man, a little bit older than me, very handsome and very poor. I fell—or thought I fell—madly in love with him. I had to have him. All my parents' arguments against him fell on deaf ears. They tried to tell me he wasn't our kind of people, that it would never work, that eventually class will tell—all that garbage I had grown to hate. I resisted their objections. They even moved us to another town trying to escape him. But that didn't work. He followed me."

She stopped at this point to take a breath and press her fingers hard against her lips. I thought she might be thinking about crying.

Finally I said, "What happened to him?"

She looked me squarely in the eye. "I married him, darling. It was your uncle Clark."

I was floored. Somehow I'd always thought of Uncle Clark as being rich. Even though Aunt Muriel always said the money was hers, I'd really had no idea he had ever been *poor.* And if he had been poor, then my mother, his sister, had been poor, too. She'd never described her past that way.

But I barely had time to reckon with that before she dropped another bombshell.

"And it was a mistake. Right from the start."

This time I couldn't hide my surprise. She read my expression and shook her head.

"Oh, no, it's not what you're thinking. I'm not going to leave him. Ever. I'm committed to him now. We have a history. And that can sometimes be an adequate substitute for love."

I said, "Aunt Muriel, why are you telling me this?"

"To illustrate a point. You see, by the looks of things, Clark has been a success. He made a great deal of money and, until lately, managed it well. But there will always be irreconcilable differences between us. Because, you see, making money does not necessarily make you wealthy. It just makes you rich. Someday you will learn that there is a difference."

I squirmed, sitting on my hands to stop myself from chewing off my nails.

"No matter what you believe, people are not the same. Those lines are drawn, and they are sharp, unforgiving lines. You cannot make them disappear."

"I don't believe that," I said.

"Oh, neither did I when I was your age. But it's true. You only have to watch people who have only known wealth and breeding their whole lives. It's in posture, gestures, movements. The truly wealthy possess something that self-made millionaires can never possess. It's called grace."

"Please," I said, thinking it was under my breath, but she heard me.

"I don't mean the kind of grace that a ballerina possesses. I mean inner grace, subtlety, a kind of peace. We have had our rough edges smoothed out. We won't grope and grasp and chase after things. We let them come to us. But people like your uncle Clark cannot stop chasing, no matter how much he gets. Money does not give him dignity. It gives him indignity. He is a slave to it."

She stood again and started pacing more slowly.

"I suppose you wonder what this is all about," she said.

"I know. You're talking about Tyler."

"Yes. I don't know anything about this young man, except that he is from hunger and that you have something akin to an obsession with him."

"I wouldn't call it that."

"I would," she said, "because I know."

"It's not the same."

"Oh, but it is. He is terribly alluring, this rootless young man. He is the perfect opportunity for you to rebel."

"I love him," I said.

"Oh my God," she gasped, then laughed. "It's like listening to myself twenty-five years ago."

"Look, I'm not saying I'll marry him," I explained, feeling like a traitor, even though Tyler and I had never discussed the M-word. "I just want to find out what happened to him."

She turned on me abruptly. "And you can't, can you?"

"N-No," I stammered.

"Why not?"

"Because his mother isn't . . . is hard to talk to, and his best friend won't listen, and—"

"He doesn't love you, Abby. So he disappeared," she said deliberately, then added, "because he can."

I stood up. I was feeling dizzy with anger.

"Why are you doing this?" I asked in a shaky voice.

"If you or Zan disappeared, there would be an entire police force and the FBI tracking you down. You cannot disappear, because you matter to too many people. But this young man possesses invisibility, and believe me, he understands the power of it."

"He matters to me," I said.

"He's gone, and you're better off letting him stay that way. I'm responsible for you, at least for the moment, and I don't want to see you go wrong. I don't want to see you make a mistake."

"Like you made?" I challenged.

"Yes," she said, not missing a beat. "Don't

do this to your parents. Don't do it to yourself. Abby, for goodness' sake, don't cross that line."

"I don't believe in lines," I declared.

I moved toward the door, but she blocked my path.

"You have no idea the damage you can cause. Be reasonable. Drop this boy. Let him disappear."

"Aunt Muriel, good night."

She stared hard at me, then her face seemed to deflate, and she moved aside to let me pass.

"I hope you will keep this conversation between us."

I looked at her.

"Why would I want to repeat it?"

For some reason, she smiled. Maybe because she misunderstood. But more likely because she understood completely.

Chapter 19

$\Longrightarrow$ I couldn't say Aunt Muriel's words didn't touch a nerve. I knew I loved Tyler passionately, but I also knew that here at the lake it was easy to feel that way. There was no one else to answer to. I couldn't be sure how I'd feel about taking him home to meet my parents. Or taking him to the prom to meet all my friends. Those images really forced me to concentrate, and ask myself how much conviction I had, and how much courage.

On the other hand, it was hard to spend much time wondering if I would take Tyler to my prom when I couldn't even be sure he was still alive. It was hard to say how committed I was to him, but I knew I was committed enough to find out what had happened to him. I owed him at least that much. When I found him I could work on answering the other questions.

That night, like the two nights before, I fell asleep with the promise of tomorrow ringing in my brain. *Tomorrow I will find him. Tomorrow all will be revealed.* I was just drifting off when a sudden crash of thunder woke me up, as if to say, "There's no time to sleep." I sat straight up, feeling pursued. But as I looked around, I could see that no one was near me except Zan, who had not stirred. I got out of my sleeping bag and walked up to the screen, staring out at the house across the cove. I thought that even if I didn't know all I knew about it, I would still sense a presence inside the house, something happening in the shadows.

Then I looked across at Tom Wheat's cabin. There was a light on inside. It must have been around one or two in the morning. I felt sorry for him, the poor man, trapped with himself and unable to sleep.

Maybe now wasn't such a good time to pay him a visit. But I felt desperate and restless, and I definitely needed to talk to someone. And if anyone were still awake at this hour, it would be Tom Wheat.

I felt around in the dark until I found my jeans and a sweatshirt. I slipped them on, trying to make as little noise as possible. But as I was zipping up my jeans, Zan stirred and came awake, raising up on her elbow.

"What are you doing?" she asked.

"Going for a walk."

"It's the middle of the night."

"I know. I can't sleep."

"But it's storming out," she said, yawning.

"I think it's going away."

"You're nuts," she said, lying back down. Then she asked, "Want me to come with you?"

"No. I want to be alone."

But this only fueled her interest. "That's not fair. You're trying to get away from me."

"I want to think."

"You can't think with me around?"

I felt across the floor for my sneakers, found them, and slipped them on.

"Look, you and I can go for a walk tomorrow. But right now I just want to wander around and think things out. It's nothing personal, all right?"

As I paused for her to answer, I heard the return of her deep and constant breathing, and I knew she had fallen back to sleep.

I went outside, closing the door softly behind me. The sky lit up and a deep rumble shook the night, making everything seem bigger and more threatening. I walked across the dark path toward Tom's cabin, trying not to think of things like snakes and wild dogs. Finally I made my way to the door of the cabin. I stood there for a while, wondering if it was completely insane to knock on his door at this hour. Then I just let myself do it without worrying about the consequences.

I stood there for a long time, waiting for an answer. Nothing happened. I held my breath and listened for noise. I couldn't hear anything. The living room light shone brightly. Maybe Tom had passed out drunk and left it on.

I knocked again, then tried the doorknob. It turned easily. I went inside and found an empty living room. Empty of people, that is. The table was littered with empty wine and champagne bottles, dirty glasses, plates with dried food on them, and stacks of paper.

"Tom?" I called softly. No answer. I made my way to the table and inspected the papers.

They were obviously pages of his novel. Some of them went on forever, others were just short pages with a few lines on them. One had an intriguing headline:

NOTES FOR A NOVEL

I read on and was even more intrigued.

GIRL AND BOY MEET AT THE LAKE, FALL IN LOVE, TROU-
BLED ROMANCE. RICH GIRL, DESTITUTE BUT ENTERPRISING LAD.
FROLICK IN THE WOODS, MAKE LOVE IN A ROW BOAT. (DISCOV-

ERED BY AN AGING WRITER——IS THIS TOO PRURIENT?) BOY
BECOMES OBSESSED WITH ACTIVITY IN EMPTY MANSION.
SYMBOLLIC OF HIS INTEREST IN WEALTH. MORE TO FOLLOW.

I folded the paper and tucked it in my back
pocket. I knew I didn't have any right to take it,
but I didn't feel that he had any right to write it.
I didn't know what bothered me more—the fact
that he was recording our lives, or the fact that
he'd described me in two short, unsympathetic
words: "rich girl." I was more than that, just as
Tyler was more than a "destitute but enterprising lad." Why did people insist on reducing everything to such simple terms?

The door to Tom's bedroom was closed. I
knocked on it, but no one answered. I opened it
and stuck my head in. He was there, lying on his
back, asleep, a book spread across his lap. An
empty champagne bottle sat on the nightstand.

"Tom," I said. "It's me. Abby Winston."

He slept on. Even though I'd never witnessed a real drunken stupor, I knew he was in
one. But I walked in anyway. I wanted to confront him.

"Look," I said, "what I told you was in confidence. You can't write about it. And even if you
do, you have to give me more credit than that.

You have to give me and Tyler more credit than that. It's serious. And I need you to help me."

He didn't stir. I moved closer to the bed and nudged him gently on the shoulder.

"Tom, come on. Wake up."

He still didn't move. I put my hand against his face, then quickly drew back, as if I'd been burned. But it wasn't warmth that made me draw back. It was cold, ice-cold, the kind I'd never felt before.

Because I'd never touched a dead person.

Chapter 20

The next morning Tom Wheat's cabin was full of policemen, moving through the house, peeking into corners, going through the garbage, taking pictures of everything. Uncle Clark spent a lot of time talking to the detective from homicide. I sat on the couch, shivering inside my sweatshirt, trying to catch bits of conversation.

"Hardly knew him," Uncle Clark said. "Just to speak to. Drank a lot. Kept to himself."

The detective nodded with a solemn expression and took notes. I stared at the bedroom door, where a lot of uniformed policemen kept passing through, and tried to erase the image of Tom lying on the bed, rigid and cold as granite. The coroner spent a long time in there, and finally came out to talk to the detective.

"Can't really tell you anything conclusive," the coroner said. He was a heavy man with gray hair and fat cheeks. He looked the way you'd think a coroner would, like someone who spent his life in a cold room, looking at dead people. "At the moment I can't find any evidence of foul play. No sign of a struggle. We tested the wineglass for suspicious substances. Nothing."

"Natural causes?" the detective asked. He, on the other hand, looked nothing like you'd think a homicide detective would. On TV they're always slightly heroic, either incredibly handsome, or respectably rumpled, like they lived and breathed for murder cases. This guy couldn't have been more than forty and was wearing a tweed jacket and jeans. He had blond, receding hair and crooked teeth. More like a high-school English teacher.

"I wouldn't say that just yet," the coroner replied. "But he did drink a lot, from what I understand, and was generally in bad health. Most likely a heart attack. I'll be able to tell more with an autopsy."

The detective nodded, scribbling away.

"Can I load him out?" the coroner asked.

Like he was talking about furniture or luggage. I shuddered.

"Sure, go ahead," said the detective.

The coroner disappeared into the bedroom again, followed by a couple of white-suited men.

The detective turned away and started

mumbling to Uncle Clark again. I strained to hear him, but all I could pick up was ". . . talk to the girl . . ."

The girl who found him. The girl who'd never seen a dead person in her life.

I'd never been, or ever expected to be, surrounded by policemen and detectives and coroners. I couldn't help wondering what my parents would think of all this. They constantly warned me and my sisters against getting into trouble. It was especially important to avoid trouble because of who my father was.

Once I was caught breaking lunch line at school. Believe it or not, this was a serious enough offense that being caught a second time would have meant suspension. A warning letter was sent home to my parents. Edwina and Leah, my younger sisters, thought this was a huge scandal. My parents gave me a sit-down talk.

"I know this doesn't seem like a big deal," my mother said. "And it wouldn't be in any other family. But your family is different."

As if I had to be told. This I knew like the back of my hand, like the Pledge of Allegiance.

"Try to avoid the little things, the petty things," my father said. "They add up."

Discovering a dead body moved me into

some other realm, something so big that I couldn't even imagine the consequences.

"Miss Winston?" came a voice. I jumped slightly.

The detective was kneeling down next to me, staring at me with a compassionate expression.

"Yes?"

"Can we talk for a second?"

"Okay," I said flatly.

"I'm Lieutenant Dillard. And you're Abby Winston, is that right?"

I nodded. I caught the eye of Uncle Clark, who was standing across the room with his arms crossed. Then I looked back at Lieutenant Dillard.

"You're Donald Winston's daughter, is that correct?"

I nodded, wondering what my father had to do with this.

"You're not going to print that, are you?" I asked.

He gave me a boyish smile. "I'm not a reporter. I don't print things."

I didn't believe him. I had been trained to fear journalists. I had been trained never to believe someone who claimed not to be a journalist.

Could I trust Lieutenant Dillard? He had a

nice face. He had a gap between his teeth. His tie was wrinkled. Were these reasons to trust a man?

"Niece of Clark Ramsey," he went on. "Fifteen years old. You reside in Washington, D.C."

"Arlington, Virginia, technically."

"Right." He wrote this down. "I understand you discovered the body."

"Yes, sir."

"This morning, around three A.M."

"I guess. I didn't know what time it was."

"Did you know Mr. Wheat?"

"A little. I mean, I just met him a few days ago."

"Then, may I ask why you were visiting him at three in the morning?"

I was stumped. I had completely forgotten how odd it looked for me to be prying around in someone's house at that time of the morning.

"I didn't do it," I said.

"Miss Winston, at this point we have no reason to suspect foul play. However, I would like to establish your relationship with the deceased, as well as your reason for being in his home at such an hour."

"I—I wanted to talk to him."

"About what?"

I caught Uncle Clark's eye again.

"I couldn't sleep."

"So you came over here."

"Well, I saw a light on. I figured he was awake."

"I see." He bit his bottom lip, staring at the floor for a long moment.

"What did you want to talk to him about?"

Here was the tricky part. Should I tell him about Tyler, or should I keep him out of it? Maybe Lieutenant Dillard could help me. But as I stared into his dull brown eyes, I got a very distinct feeling that even though he might be interested in Tyler's case, he wouldn't understand. Anyway, if Tyler had just taken off of his own accord, I didn't want to drag him into this mess.

"Just things in general. He was great at talking. He said the most incredible things."

I allowed myself to say these things, feeling like I was giving him a eulogy rather than divulging secrets.

"Like what?" Lieutenant Dillard asked, smiling.

"Well, he was a writer, so he mostly talked about writing."

"Anything else? I mean, did he ever say anything that made you think he was . . . despondent?"

"He didn't kill himself," I said quickly.

"No, you're probably right. I'm just trying to get an idea of his mood before he died. When was the last time you saw him?"

"The day before yesterday."

"And he seemed in good spirits?"

"I guess."

"Was he drinking?"

I hesitated.

Lieutenant Dillard, who was a quick guy, said, "The autopsy will reveal the alcohol level in his blood."

"Yes," I said. "He was always drinking."

"And what did the two of you talk about?"

"I gave him something to keep for me."

"What?"

"A backpack."

This just came out. As soon as I said it, I knew I shouldn't have.

"Whose backpack?"

"Mine," I said quickly. "I wanted him to keep it for me."

"Why?"

"I just wanted him to."

"What was in it?"

"Just some clothes and stuff."

He raised his thin eyebrows at me, and I could see he was not going to let it go at that.

"And a bottle of wine," I said.

"Oh, really?"

"Well, you know, I'm underage. I wanted him to hide it for me."

This seemed to satisfy him. He nodded, pinching his lips together.

"Well, that's strange," he said.

"Why?"

"Because I've got a list of his personal belongings here, and there's nothing about a backpack."

"I'm sure he hid it," I said.

"We made a very thorough search."

"I don't know," I said, feeling my heart speed up. "I gave it to him."

He nodded again, staring hard at me. But I wasn't thinking about him anymore. I was thinking of the backpack, wondering why it had disappeared.

"Just one more thing, Miss Winston. When you last spoke to him, did he seem agitated in any way? Fearful, anxious?"

"No."

"Sure about that?"

"Yes." I remembered him as I last saw him, as I always saw him, half-drunk and happy.

"Okay," he said, rising. "I think that's all we

need. We'll contact you if we think of anything else."

I nodded, and he gave me a smile before he walked away. Uncle Clark came over then and sat beside me on the couch.

"You all right?" he asked, putting a hand on my shoulder.

I nodded.

"You liked him, didn't you?" he asked, meaning Tom.

"Yes."

"Well, you've had a hard day. Let's go back and put you to bed."

"Okay."

He stood and offered a hand to me. I took it and let him pull me off the couch. I felt like a sack of flour, heavy and clumsy.

"What did he ask you?"

"Nothing, really," I said. "Just how I knew Tom, what his mood was like, that kind of thing."

"What did you tell him?"

"Only what I knew. It wasn't much."

Uncle Clark put his arm around me and patted my shoulder. As we walked together out of the house, I couldn't get my mind to stop whirling with questions.

Where was the backpack?

Where was Tyler?

Why did Tom Wheat die?

I didn't know anything at all, except that the answers were somehow connected.

Chapter 21

"Of all the stupid luck," Zan grumbled. "We finally get two weeks at the lake and somebody has to go and die."

"Alexandria, that is a reprehensible attitude," Uncle Clark said.

"I know, Daddy, but we've only got three days left."

We were trying to have lunch, eating peanut butter and banana sandwiches out on the porch. No one had much of an appetite, least of all me. I sat and stared at my bread, taking long, slow breaths. Outside the lake looked raw and wild after the rains, sloshing against the shore.

"Well, at least she's honest," Aunt Muriel said. "I think we're all feeling that way to a certain extent."

"I'm not, and Abby certainly isn't," said Uncle Clark, taking a sip of wine.

"It doesn't mean we don't feel bad for that

poor man. But let's face it, our vacation is ruined," said Aunt Muriel.

I released another sigh, which made Aunt Muriel pat me on the arm.

"And Abby may never get over this," she said.

"There is one thing I still don't understand," said Uncle Clark. "Just what were you doing in that man's house at that hour?"

"I don't know. I felt like talking to somebody."

"You could have talked to me," Zan said. "I was awake."

"I can't explain it. Please don't make me."

Uncle Clark said, "Does this have to do with that young man, Tyler Crane?"

"No," I lied.

"You weren't meeting him over there, were you?"

"I haven't seen him since last week. He's gone."

"Disappeared," Aunt Muriel reminded Uncle Clark in a ponderous tone.

"Abby, I don't know what to say. I'm sorry for what you've been through. But I can't say I like the way you have deliberately jeopardized your father's reputation by putting yourself into ignominious situations," Uncle Clark said sternly.

"Oh, don't be so hard on her," Aunt Muriel implored. "She's a teenager, Clark. She's going to do foolish things."

"I guess this means we can't take the boat out," Zan said.

"Don't you think that would be a little tasteless?" Aunt Muriel said.

"I didn't even know him!" Zan said.

"He was still our neighbor."

"Besides," Uncle Clark said, "I told the lieutenant I'd stay close by, in case he needed to ask any more questions."

Aunt Muriel looked alarmed.

"Surely they don't suspect us of anything."

"Of course they don't, Muriel. He probably died of natural causes. It's just that we are his neighbors, and I volunteered to help in any way that I could."

"Thanks a lot, Daddy," Zan said.

"Young lady, I'd very much like you to go inside before I lose my temper."

Zan lowered her head, looking humble. "I'm sorry. I'm just disappointed."

Uncle Clark nodded. "Go to your room anyway. You need to settle down."

Zan obeyed. It surprised me to see her acting

so submissive, but I knew we were all a little shaken up and disoriented.

"Are you all right, Abby?" Uncle Clark asked.

"Yes, sir."

It was about the tenth time he'd asked, but in a way I appreciated it.

Suddenly there was the sound of tires on gravel. Aunt Muriel got up and went to look out the screen door. She turned back to us with a worried expression.

"Clark, it's the police."

"Nothing to worry about, Muriel. Just tying up loose ends, I'm sure."

But I could see that Uncle Clark was none too calm himself.

Lieutenant Dillard tapped on the door, and Aunt Muriel let him in, offering him something to drink before he could even say hello. He declined.

"I'm here to talk to your husband, Mrs. Ramsey."

"Yes. Of course."

Lieutenant Dillard looked less together than the last time I'd seen him. His wrinkled tie was now loosened, his top button undone. His hair had started to curl in the heat. He looked very harried, and this made me nervous.

"If we could have a moment alone?" he said, nodding at my uncle.

"Absolutely," said Aunt Muriel.

She went inside, and I'd started in that direction when Lieutenant Dillard stopped me.

"You can stay, Miss Winston."

"Is that wise?" Uncle Clark asked.

"Well, she is the one who found the deceased. There's really no way to protect her from this now. I'm sorry."

Uncle Clark nodded. I sat back down.

Lieutenant Dillard took out a little notepad, glanced at it, and started talking.

"The autopsy report was a bit puzzling. There was no scarring on the coronary tissue, which means he did not die of a heart attack. He appeared to be in pretty good health for a fifty-two-year-old man. There was an exceptionally high level of alcohol in his bloodstream, but insufficient to cause death, and no other suspicious substances were found."

Lieutenant Dillard paused, as if he was waiting for one of us to say something.

"How did he die?" Uncle Clark finally asked.

"The oxygen supply to the brain was cut off for a substantial period of time."

"You mean he just stopped breathing?"

"Or was caused to stop."

Uncle Clark looked at me briefly, then back at Lieutenant Dillard.

"He was strangled?"

Lieutenant Dillard shook his head. "Suffocated. Most likely with a pillow. We found cotton fibers around his mouth, and a piece of down in his larynx. It was consistent with the feathers in the pillows on his bed."

"I don't understand. Are you saying he suffocated *himself* somehow?"

"Oh, no. I'm not saying that at all."

Uncle Clark gave me another look. I couldn't do anything but stare back at him. If he expected me to be surprised, I disappointed him.

"It makes no sense," Uncle Clark said. "Who would want to murder that man? He seemed so harmless."

"I don't know, sir. But that's what we intend to find out."

Lieutenant Dillard looked at me then.

"Miss Winston, are you absolutely certain you've told us everything you know."

"He was dead when I found him," I said.

"We're not accusing you of anything," he said.

"I should hope not," Uncle Clark said angrily.

"Please, Mr. Ramsey, don't take this personally. I am only doing my job."

"She's a child, for Christ's sake!"

Lieutenant Dillard let a quiet moment pass, then turned to me again. "You're sure you didn't see anyone entering or leaving the house?"

As nervous as I was, this made me like Lieutenant Dillard more. He had ignored Uncle Clark's claim that I was a child. He looked at me as if to say we both knew better.

"No, sir," I said.

"And you can't think of any reason that someone would want to murder Tom Wheat?"

That was a tricky question. I could think of a lot of strange things—Tom's connection to Tyler, the missing backpack, the house across the cove—but none of them added up to a good reason for killing a man.

So I answered honestly, "No, I can't."

He moved closer to me and knelt down. My heart was beating hard with hope. Maybe he had discovered something which would lead to Tyler. I no longer cared about my parents and any scandal that this would provoke. I only cared about Tyler.

"It seems to me that you have something on your mind. I wish you'd share it with me. I promise, you're not in any kind of trouble. No one suspects you of anything. And all of this information is confidential."

"I . . ."

It was so tempting to blurt out all my concerns to him. Uncle Clark's cool blue eyes met with mine. I could have sworn there was a warning in them.

"I've told you everything I know."

Lieutenant Dillard and I locked eyes for what seemed like forever, then I buried my face in my hands. It was all getting to be too much.

"I think that's enough," Uncle Clark said.

When I looked up again Lieutenant Dillard was at the door.

"I don't like this part of my job any more than you do, Mr. Ramsey. But this is a murder investigation now. We can't protect anyone, even minors."

Uncle Clark said, "I appreciate that. But I also have to look out for my niece. Her father is a very influential and respectable man. I'd hate to put his career in jeopardy. So please don't bother us again until you have more to go on than a feather in someone's throat."

Lieutenant Dillard smirked.

"You've been very helpful."

With that, Lieutenant Dillard went outside, letting the door slam behind him.

"Are you all right?" Uncle Clark asked me.

"Yes."

"I'm sorry you had to go through that."

I shrugged. Our eyes connected. We had the same eyes, the same dull blue-gray that came from my mother's side of the family. We were of the same blood—cut from the same cloth, as Tom Wheat would have said.

Uncle Clark gave me a reassuring smile, then went inside.

I waited until I heard the door to his office close before I ran outside to catch Lieutenant Dillard.

Chapter 22

He was starting his car when he saw me running toward him. He quickly cut the engine off and got out.

"You've thought of something else?" he asked.

He looked so unthreatening and familiar, like a teacher asking why I had missed a test, that I couldn't even bring myself to be nervous. Somewhere along the line I had changed. Somewhere between seeing his loosened tie and looking into my uncle's eyes, I had switched allegiances. I trusted Lieutenant Dillard.

So I told him all about me and Tyler, how he had suspected something was going on at the house across the cove, and how he had disappeared so suddenly, and all about our friendship with Tom Wheat. He listened, nodding occasionally, stopping now and then to jot a note on his pad.

"And the backpack?" he said to me.

"Oh, that. I found it in Tyler's trailer. I gave it to Tom for safekeeping."

"But it seems to have disappeared."

"Yes, that's right."

"Tell me exactly what was in there."

"Just some of Tyler's clothes and stuff. But that's the whole point. It belonged to Tyler. And now he's missing, and so is his backpack."

"You said something about a bottle of wine."

"Yes, that was in there, too."

"Yours?"

"No, Tyler's." I paused, wondering if I should reveal more. Lieutenant Dillard trained his eyes on me, waiting.

"Actually, it belonged to my uncle Clark. I mean, it came from his winery."

His thin eyebrows went up. He suddenly seemed very interested. Why, I thought? What does this have to do with my uncle? It was as if a suspicion had already been planted in the lieutenant's mind, and I was bringing it to life.

"I think that's just a coincidence," I said. "Uncle Clark has several cases of wine in the house. He might have given a bottle to Tyler. He probably did, because Tyler complimented him on it once. He's always passing it out to people."

Lieutenant Dillard scribbled on his pad, then looked up at me with a serious expression. He no longer looked like a simple English teacher. He was sharp and on the ball, someone you couldn't keep secrets from.

"You think someone took the backpack because of the wine?" he asked.

"No. I think they took it because of Tyler. Because of what he knew."

"What he knew?"

"About the house across the cove."

Lieutenant Dillard looked in that direction. From where we were standing you could only make out the front porch through the trees, and the chimney jutting above the cluster of green leaves.

"Who does that house belong to?"

"A Dr. Kaplan. I don't know anything about him, except that he's never lived there. The house is empty."

"Not according to your friend Tyler."

"Yes, well . . ." I didn't know what to say.

Lieutenant Dillard said, "Crane, Crane. What's his father's name?"

"I don't know."

"Not Reginald Crane?"

I shrugged.

"An insurance man?"

I nodded slowly.

"He was an old acquaintance of mine," said

Lieutenant Dillard. "Saw him all the time at the coffee shop. Very nice man. Killed himself, you know. Recently."

"Yes, I know."

He stared at me for a moment, and I read his expression.

"Tyler wasn't crazy," I said.

" 'Wasn't'?"

"Isn't. If he's alive."

"What makes you think he isn't?"

I looked at the ground for a moment. A caterpillar was crawling slowly across a leaf, toward my foot.

"Do me a favor," I said. "Call his friend Rod Stone. He knew Tyler better than anybody. He knew how worried he was about the house and all."

"Rod Stone? Bill Stone's boy?"

I nodded. "He works at Castle Hardware."

"Thank you for telling me this," he said, but he didn't write any of it down.

"Does it help?" I asked.

He opened the car door. "I don't know. Probably not. You'd be surprised. Murders aren't usually this complicated. That's what people don't really understand. Ninety percent of all murders are crimes of passion. It takes a rare mind to sit down and calculate something like that. It takes an even rarer one to come up with something too clever for homicide. I suspect when we find an answer to this case, it will be a lot simpler than any of us has imagined."

"What about Tyler?" I asked as he slid into the driver's seat.

He shrugged. "We'll look into it, but . . ."

"But what?"

"Before I made lieutenant I answered a few calls on him myself."

"For what?" I asked, my heart pounding.

"Disappearing," he said.

I grabbed the door before he could close it.

"This is different," I said.

But Lieutenant Dillard only smiled at me and closed the door.

When I came back into the cabin, Uncle Clark was sitting in a chair, staring at his fingers, drumming a silent beat across his thighs.

I stood still in the doorway and looked at him.

"I don't understand," he said, staring at his knees. "I work so hard to protect you. Then you do everything you can to sabotage it."

"I . . . needed to tell him something."

"Do you think it's easy? Working your way from a humble beginning to the position I'm in today?"

I said nothing.

"It doesn't happen overnight. But destroying it, that can happen in a blink of an eye."

"I'm sorry," I said.

He stood and walked toward me, his gray eyes bearing down hard on my face. I couldn't look away.

"We're innocent," I said in a shaky voice. "We don't have anything to worry about."

"There is *always* something to worry about," he said slowly, deliberately.

"Like what?"

"Abigail," he said, and I shuddered at the sound of my full name. "I am a well-respected citizen in a small community. I rely on my reputation to keep my businesses alive. I can't even afford to get a speeding ticket, and now I am mixed up in murder. Why would you make matters worse by associating my family with this Crane boy?"

"I love him," I said weakly.

"That's preposterous. His family is completely unstable. You must know that!"

He took me by the shoulders and shook me slightly.

"Listen to me. Love only lasts for a second; your reputation lasts forever. Long after this boy is forgotten, everything you've said will live on and on. I can't believe you'd risk so much for a boy you hardly know!"

I turned my eyes away then. I couldn't stand it anymore. The things he said were hurting me. And I was more than a little bit scared.

He let go of me. My arms felt bruised where he had gripped them. I wanted to rub them, but I was still afraid of him.

"This won't go away," he said. "Not for a long time."

I closed my eyes and counted silently to ten. When I opened them he was gone.

Chapter 23

For the first time since I could remember, Zan chose not to sleep on the porch and went inside to one of the guest rooms. She asked me to join her, but I said no. I wanted to be alone, close to the water, closer somehow to Tyler. And I wanted to think.

Eventually I got up, put on my jeans, and walked down to the dock. I wanted to sit on those boards that Tyler had nailed together. Now that Tom was dead, this was my last connection to Tyler. I had no idea when or if I would ever see him again, but I could sit here, where he had worked, looking at the nails he had placed, the boards he had made sturdy for us. I remembered him that day, his back turned to the sun, his hands working steadily and, when he looked at me, his nose a soft pink. "Love at first sight" didn't necessarily mean anything to most people. But to me, it did. This feeling, faint as it was and getting fainter—this feeling was the only thing I could trust.

Still, I allowed myself a moment to be sensible. My parents were big on being sensible. My father always said, "When in doubt, always give reason a chance." So I tried to picture my life back home. If I could just let a few days pass, I could get back to all that was familiar and normal.

I could see myself back in Arlington, with all the usual sights and sounds—the cars passing quietly on our cul-de-sac, classical music playing on my mother's stereo, my sisters bickering. I could see myself back with the old crowd, hanging out at Springfield Mall, standing in line at Ticketmaster for the concerts we wanted to see. Going back to school and sneaking glances at all the good-looking guys. Everyone would look vaguely alike—the guys all wearing oversized T-shirts or oxford cloth shirts and Levi's and stark white sneakers, the girls all dressed in whatever they thought the boys wanted to see. The rule would be sameness.

The only thing that would distinguish me, make me stand out in this sea of sameness, was what had happened to me this summer. I had fallen in love with a guy so unlike me that it was a struggle to put him into the picture of my life. The death of Tom Wheat, the investigation, meeting Lieutenant Dillard—all these strange occurrences could be swept away. I could lose all of this, and maybe a smarter person would want it that way, I told myself. I knew it would be easy to let my old life take over, and that if I did, all this would fade and disappear. Or become the subject of an English essay. "What I Did with My Summer."

This made me think of my English teacher, Mrs. Todd, who taught us about the elements one needed to construct a story. She said that a character must get from point A to point C by overcoming an obstacle in the middle, which was point B. In the process the character changes, or does not change. Not changing, she said, is a story, too. But she knew, and now I understood, that not changing was always a sadder story.

I let my eyes wander across the lake. The House was as dark as ever, its windows like sightless eyes peering out at nothing.

I had made up my mind what to do. I went directly to the rowboat and began unmooring it. It was difficult, because it was dark and the knot was tied firmly—one of Uncle Clark's special knots. He didn't like anyone but him taking the boats out, so he always tied them in a way that none of us could undo. But I had all night, and determination was on my side.

I was starting to make some headway when I heard the soft sound of footsteps nearby. I froze. The sound of my own breathing pounded in my ears.

"What in the world are you doing?"

I looked up. A dark shape was outlined in the pale moonlight.

"Nothing," I said.

"Doesn't look like nothing to me."

Aunt Muriel walked onto the dock. She was wearing jeans and a windbreaker, all her makeup and jewelry still on. Obviously I wasn't the only one who couldn't sleep.

"I'm taking the boat out," I said.

"Don't be ridiculous. It's the middle of the night."

"There's something I have to do. Please don't try to stop me."

"But Abby, it's dangerous. Rowing out in the middle of a dark lake, all by yourself? If anything happened to you . . ."

"It won't."

She stared at me for a moment. "You're going to that house, aren't you."

"I have to."

She put an arm around me and gave me a hard hug.

"Poor Abby. You've really had a bad time of it, haven't you. I'm so sorry all this happened to you. But you're in shock. You're not behaving rationally."

I said, "Aunt Muriel, something is going on. I don't know what, but I've got to find out. Tom Wheat was murdered."

Her eyes widened.

"Clark didn't tell me that."

"No, he wouldn't," I said quietly.

"Why not?"

I couldn't tell her. If she didn't already think I was crazy, my latest theory would surely convince her. No, the only hope was to get inside that house and look around, find out what Tyler had discovered, and come back with some kind of tangible proof. It was the only way that anyone would ever believe me. With some kind of evidence, I could go back to Lieutenant Dillard and persuade him to look for Tyler.

"This is something I have to do, Aunt Muriel," I said, then turned my attention back to the knot.

"You'll never get it," she said. "It's Clark's secret knot."

"I'll get it."

"Oh, Abby, don't be foolish. Listen to reason. You could get hurt. You can't go alone."

I ignored her and went on struggling.

"Well, if you insist on going, then I'll have to go with you."

I looked at her. She seemed to be serious.

"Do you want to?" I asked.

"Of course I don't want to. I'd rather go inside and mix a martini. But if anything happened to you, I'd never be able to live with myself."

I considered it. It seemed like a good solution. Having a witness with me could only help my case.

"All right," I said. "Help me with this knot."

She took over, and in a second she had the knot untied.

She smiled at me. "We've been married twenty-two years. He can't keep secrets from me."

Aunt Muriel and I took turns rowing. It was a long process, and she passed the time by telling me stories of reckless things she did when she was a teenager. The stories were all somehow unoriginal—drag racing, shoplifting, jump-starting cars. The teenage escapades of adults always sounded unreal to me. It occurred to me briefly that one day, this story might seem unreal to a child of mine: "Then there was the time your father disappeared and I rowed across the lake to look for clues," I imagined myself saying to a daughter with Tyler's big brown eyes. It didn't matter to me that she wouldn't believe it, only that Tyler and I would both live long enough to make it happen.

Aunt Muriel stared intently at the distant shore and continued rowing toward it at a leisurely pace. My mouth was so dry, I wasn't sure I could form a sentence if I suddenly had to.

"I know I've given you all this sage advice," Aunt Muriel said, "but the truth is, I know exactly how you feel. I did love Clark once; I'm sure I didn't imagine it. And I don't really know what came between us. These things happen, almost without you noticing."

I looked over my shoulder.

"Is he asleep?"

"Yes, I think so. I didn't see a light on in his office."

The house was getting closer, but no friendlier. It still looked dark and threatening. My heart was pounding so hard it almost stole my breath.

"You really do think there is some mystery to all this?" Aunt Muriel asked.

"Yes."

"But this is Flanders Lake. Bolwood Cove. Nothing mysterious happens here. Who would be behind something like murder and missing teenagers?"

"I don't know. Maybe Dr. Kaplan."

She laughed. "Oh, mercy, that's a good one. Old Kap. He can't even make himself go to work, let alone murder anyone. He spends all his time on vacation and on the golf course. I assure you, it would take much more energy than he has to do something like that."

"I don't know. Can't you row any faster?"

Aunt Muriel gave another big heave and edged the boat forward.

"I must be out of my mind," she said. "I could be in bed."

We finally reached the dock, and I moored the boat. Aunt Muriel got out first and helped me. We stood on the dock, staring up at the dark house.

"No one home," Aunt Muriel said.

"We'll see about that."

"Yes, and just what do we do if someone is at home? Say, 'Excuse us, we're just looking for a murderer'?"

"I'll think of something."

The front door was locked, and I didn't have anything with me to pick the lock with. I cursed myself for not bringing a knife, a nail file, anything sharp.

Aunt Muriel said, "What about the back?"

"Let's try it."

We made our way around the side of the house. I listened for any kind of strange sounds, but I couldn't hear anything but night birds and the distant slosh of the lake.

The back door was locked, too, but the window in the kitchen had been smashed in. It looked big enough for me to crawl through.

"Your sweetheart did that," Aunt Muriel said, "according to Clark."

"You wait here. I'll let you in."

"This is nonsense, Abby," she said, but the excited tone of her voice made me think she was almost enjoying the adventure.

I made my way through the small space, taking care not to cut myself on any loose pieces of glass. I landed in the kitchen. It was completely dark and empty. The only footsteps on the floor were the muddy ones I had just made. I went over and opened the back door for Aunt Muriel, who came inside and looked around cautiously.

"You know, I've never seen the inside of Kap's house before. Not bad."

"I'll look through the living room," I said. "You look upstairs."

"What is it we're looking *for*?" she asked, following me.

"Anything."

"Well, that makes it easier."

She reached for a light switch.

"Don't," I said.

"Why on earth not? I can't see a thing."

"We don't want to let anyone know we're here."

"Who's looking?"

I thought about Uncle Clark, how easily he might see a light pop on in the window from across the cove.

"Just to be safe," I said.

"Oh, all right. But if I break my leg, I'll have a hard time explaining it."

She moved off toward the stairs and I went into the living room. There was nothing in it but an old telephone. I picked it up and heard a buzzing sound in my ear. It surprised me that there would be a working phone in an abandoned place like this. I hung up, then made my way over to a closet. I opened the door cautiously; it was so new it didn't even creak. The closet was empty. I closed it again and walked across the empty room, my footsteps echoing loudly across the bare wood floor.

I noticed another door and moved toward it. This door wasn't a closet. This door led somewhere, like to a basement.

I put my hand on the knob, hoping that I was about to open the door that would reveal the answers to my questions. I felt like a contestant on a game show. Inside would either be my dream car or a donkey, the dud prize for which I had foolishly risked everything.

The door was locked.

Aunt Muriel came around the corner and found me tugging furiously on the doorknob, something I had resorted to for lack of options.

"I don't think you're getting anywhere," she observed.

"Do you have a knife or anything? A nail file?"

"No."

"Maybe there's something in the kitchen."

As I started in that direction, she reached out and grabbed my arm.

"Don't," she said.

"What?"

"Don't," she repeated. "We should not open that door."

"We're already trespassing. What difference will one more door make?"

I kept walking, and just as I reached the entrance to the kitchen, she said behind me in a low, cool voice, "One door could make a very *big* difference."

I turned and looked at her from across the room. The pale moonlight falling on her skin made her look like a skeleton.

I froze in place, feeling my limbs turning numb.

It hit me suddenly. The crates, the wine, the break-ins at the winery. All of this had something to do with Uncle Clark. All this time, the mystery hadn't been across the water; it had been right under my nose.

Aunt Muriel walked slowly but steadily across the room, her eyes fixed on me. By the time she reached me, I understood. In the basement, under the floorboards where her feet touched down as quietly as a cat's, were the secrets. Secrets put there not by strange men in masks or Dr. Kaplan or ancient ghosts. Secrets put there by my own family.

That was the last thing I had time to think before my head swirled, everything blurred, and my legs abandoned me.

Chapter 24

When I came to, I was lying on the living room floor, something soft under my head. The something soft, I saw as I craned my neck, was Aunt Muriel's jacket. I tried not to receive the thoughts that were coming at me like a freight train.

Aunt Muriel was standing by the window, staring out at the lake and smoking a cigarette. She must have heard me move, because she whirled around quickly.

"You're awake," she said.

"I guess."

"You fainted. I thought you might be in shock. I didn't know how to revive you. Does your head hurt? That jacket is the only thing I could find—"

"What's going on?" I asked, rising on my elbows.

"Don't get up too fast. You may get dizzy."

"Aunt Muriel, tell me."

She turned back to the window for a moment, finishing her cigarette and stubbing it on the floor.

"Poor Abby. It's so unfortunate. You're drawn to strays, just as I was. I tried to warn you, they can only lead to trouble. But I suppose I had forgotten the particular hardness of a fifteen-year-old head."

In a quieter voice she added, "And the softness of a fifteen-year-old heart."

"What's in the basement?"

She smiled at me, a sad smile, then began to pace leisurely across the room, as if she had nowhere to go and nothing to do but talk.

"You never knew my father. You couldn't. He died before you were born. He was an exceptional man. Shrewd, creative, inventive, some said brilliant. He could be kind, and he could be ruthless. It all depended on how he felt about you.

"Well, how my father felt about me was disappointed. He wanted a fleet of sons, but as fate decreed it, he was only given a single daughter. Never mind that I was smart and ambitious. I was female, and that was my sin. He never forgave me for it.

"As I tried to tell you earlier, my attachment to Clark was an effort to rebel against his tyranny. There was always the danger of marrying someone my father would actually prefer to me. I thought that would never happen if I married Clark. In fact, I thought it might make my father see me in a new light. That he would somehow be motivated to turn his businesses over to me instead of to his son-in-law. No such luck. A smart female was never a match for the most dull-witted male. He passed the mills on to Clark. I was supposed to take my place in the shadows, the place I had occupied since birth.

"As for Clark, he truly has absolutely no business sense. That became apparent right away. But like most men of his time, he refused to listen to any woman's advice. So over the years he began to let our fortune dwindle away. His final act of stupidity was that winery. It was frivolity on his part, an expensive toy. But I knew right away it was going to sink us."

She stopped talking and turned to me with a sincere expression, as if she were sharing a secret.

"A person who has always had money cannot embrace poverty. It is a kind of death. So any kind of action I took to avoid it seemed worth the risk. There is nothing quite so dangerous, or unstoppable, as a person with nothing to lose."

The words sent a chill through me. It all made a perfectly eerie kind of sense. I couldn't argue with her.

"Are you comfortable?" she asked me suddenly.

"Y-Yes."

"Good." She took a deep breath, then began to pace again. "On the night that his winery opened, Clark threw a party. A celebration. Celebrating our descent into destitution, I suppose. Anyway, it was at this party that I met up with our old friend Dr. Kaplan. Kap. I had known him for years. Kap and I had a special bond—we were both being ruined by our spouses. His wife was a free spender. She was the one who talked him into building this monstrosity that he couldn't afford. I knew he was suffering from financial difficulties. I'd heard it through the usual grapevine. I had had a lot to drink, and I started to talk to him about increasing—actually saving—each of our incomes. I spoke to him in veiled language, but he understood.

"It was his idea. I don't blame it all on him, but he took the ball and ran with it. He had a brilliant little scheme with low risk and high reward. My father had warned me against such notions, but Kap made it sound so perfect. 'I've got some boys who'll do the work,' he said. 'Clark will never know. Sherlock Holmes couldn't trace it to us.' 'Trace what?' I asked, and that was when he spelled out a simple little plan to rob the winery. He'd smuggle the wine out of the country, probably to Mexico, and sell it there. Clark and I would collect the insurance money. Soon the winery would fail, but we'd be out of the hole, and Kap would make a tidy little profit for himself. All I had to do was supply him with the security code to the winery.

"It sounded so neat and easy. No one was paying any attention to Clark's wine. Right after he went into production with his famous patented wine bottle, scientific research proved that this vessel had absolutely no effect on the quality of the wine. So what we had was a worthless bottle full of worthless wine. The best thing to do was have someone rip him off, collect the insurance money, and let the whole enterprise die a slow and respectable death."

She looked away from me then, pinching her lip, as if the rest of the story were too painful to repeat.

"So there was one robbery, then another and another. Then more. Clark refused to close the place, and the robberies continued. All the while, I noticed that Kap was staying out of the country for longer and longer periods of time. He went into semiretirement. Where was all his money coming from? I knew he couldn't make enough money selling bootleg wine to stay in the Bahamas for life. So I confronted him, nagging and threatening until he told me the truth. The wine was being sold, but not for the going rate. No, it was selling for something way beyond that. Because the doctor wasn't selling bottles of wine. He was filling the bottles with a much more valuable commodity."

She waited for a moment, holding for the answer, as if building up to the punch line of a joke.

"Liquid morphine," she said quietly.

I stared at her, too numb with horror to say anything.

"Take some liquid morphine," she said, "add a few drops of red food coloring, and suddenly you have a very marketable product indeed. Morphine is extremely addictive, and I'm sure Kap's customers paid whatever he asked."

"But it's *drugs*."

"I know that. I hated it. But what could I do? To paraphrase the good doctor, I was already in it, up to my neck. In a court of law he could prove I was a part of the whole scheme. How else could he have gotten the security code?"

She saw the way I was looking at her and shook her head. "I know it's awful. I knew it then. But I didn't know how to get out, Abby. I honestly didn't. Daddy used to say, 'It's okay to change horses in the middle of a stream . . . as long as you're getting on a better horse.' The problem was, I didn't even *have* a horse, let alone a better one."

She laughed and waited for me to do the same. I'd obviously missed the joke, and my stony expression stopped her laughter short. She went on.

"I forced myself to stop thinking about it. I separated myself. I entered a state of denial. My only goal was survival.

"If I had less of a conscience, I'd have appreciated how perfect the plan was. The only stumbling block had been how to transport it. Using Kap's house as a temporary storage place was a stroke of genius. An empty house. No neighbors. No one had been near it since it was built. And

Kap himself would be in the Bahamas. No one could possibly connect either of us to it."

She shook her head and smiled, staring at a distant wall. "Until your young man came along."

"What have you done with Tyler?" I asked. It was the only question I cared about.

"I didn't like him, Abby. I never liked him. He wasn't good enough for you. He was an opportunist, just like Clark was. Don't you see I was trying to help? I was trying to protect you. I didn't want you to end up like me!"

"What have you done with him?"

"Imagine how I felt when our employees called me up to say someone had been snooping around, breaking in. Imagine how I felt when that boy came and told Clark everything. Everything. Do you know how hard I had to work to get Clark to ignore him? Clark actually wanted to call the police. 'Oh, yes,' I said, 'and get ourselves involved in some crazy story about ghosts and missing persons? A lot of good that would do for your business.' You could always sway Clark with a threat against his business."

She fixed her eyes on the wall again, and seemed to drift into a reverie. Then she turned to me, her eyes wide, with a sudden but important thought.

"I never did mean to hurt anyone. Honestly. I'm not the kind of person who can give pain. Even the morphine . . . well, drugs are designed to *stop* pain, aren't they? That's what I told myself. I really never thought I'd have to—"

She stopped, bringing her fists against her temples, as if trying to press out a bad memory.

"I hate that part. I hate it," she said.

"You killed Tom Wheat," I said.

Her expression changed. It was as if I could actually see the child in her emerging. She looked miserable, and for a moment I thought she might cry.

This was the moment where I told myself no, I don't believe it; this is not my aunt, not Zan's mother.

"I really didn't mean to," she said. "I went over to see him that night, right after our talk. Went out the back way, so no one would see me. The light was still on; I figured he was awake, and I could talk to him. The door was open, so I walked in. And there he was, lying on his bed, passed out drunk. I nudged him, tried to wake him up, but he was out cold.

"I fully intended to walk away. But then I saw the backpack. Lying by his bed. I had a feeling it didn't belong to him. I looked in it, and right away I found the wine. That was when I realized something. He had to go."

She paused, as if to remember some detail.

"It was so easy. Simple. The pillow was there, he was unconscious, he never even knew what hit him. He went to sleep and never woke up."

"How could you do that, Aunt Muriel?" I asked in a quiet voice.

She turned to me, suddenly angry.

"You're the one who gave him the backpack. So it's your fault, too. I found that out from Clark. He overheard what you said to the police. Poor, dumb Clark. He knew the whole story, but he didn't understand any of it."

She smiled.

"Do you see what I'm saying now? I'm smarter than he is. I always have been."

I just nodded. My mouth was dry. But there were two questions I had to ask, even though I was afraid of the answers.

"Did you kill Tyler?" I asked flatly, hating the sound of it.

This she didn't answer. She turned away

from me and stared out at the lake, her back as stiff as a board.

"Are you going to kill me?" I asked quietly.

Still she didn't move.

After a moment she sighed. "Oh, Abby, it's so complicated. I don't know what to do. There was a time when I literally would not have killed a cricket, a spider, anything. I used to make Clark rescue insects from the bath and send them back out into their world. To deprive something of its consciousness seemed unthinkable. But that was all so long ago."

"You love me, though," I said.

"Yes, of course. You're my niece and I love you. But there is Zan. I love her more. I'd do anything to keep her safe and unharmed."

"What if I promised to keep quiet?"

She didn't seem to be hearing me.

"I could lock you up. That would be all right for now. Just to give me some time to think. Yes, I have to be able to think."

She moved toward me and I backed away, sliding across the bare floor.

"I'm not going to hurt you. I'm just going to put you away somewhere."

"Please, don't. You're not well, Aunt Muriel.

You're not yourself. If we can get you somewhere, they'll help. They'll explain it all."

"Who's 'they,' Abby? Doctors? Do you
think I'm crazy? That I don't have control of
this situation? Don't you see I have to do this?
Listen to me! I don't have a choice!"

I was trying to escape her, but her hard,
strong fingers had closed around my shoulders. I
kept squirming, because I couldn't stand the
thought of being locked up, forgotten, maybe
even left to die. If she would kill Tom Wheat
and Tyler, why wouldn't she kill me? It mattered that I was her niece, but it wouldn't matter
for long. She said it herself—there was nothing
so unstoppable as a person with nothing to lose.

Despite my resistance, she lifted me up off
the floor and dragged me toward the door, the
one I suspected led to a basement. Now I was
certain—she was going to put me down there
and leave me. Then *I* would be the secret. The
secret in the house across the cove.

She unlocked the door and told me to open
it. I said no, and her fingers closed even harder.
She was hurting me. I didn't know what else to
do, so I turned the knob. I opened it and saw a
staircase leading down into damp darkness.

She pushed me a little, and I pictured myself

falling down the stairs, into nothing but endless space, like a black hole.

I must have heard all the sounds—the car engine, the door opening, the scuffling of feet—but I didn't put any of it together until I heard the voice.

"Let her go. Let the girl go, Mrs. Ramsey. We've got you covered."

Chapter 25

At the time it seemed like there were dozens of people surrounding us, an entire SWAT team, all with high-powered rifles pointing in our direction. After my eyes adjusted to the light, I realized there were only two blue-uniformed policemen with revolvers, accompanied by Lieutenant Dillard and Rod Stone. I stared hard at their faces, trying to place them. I knew them, yet my brain wouldn't work. I couldn't understand where they had come from.

"Don't shoot," I pleaded.

"Let her go, Mrs. Ramsey," a policeman ordered.

To my surprise, Aunt Muriel began to laugh.

"Oh, for heaven's sake. I wouldn't hurt this girl. She's my niece. We were only playing a kind of game. Tell them, Abby."

I couldn't say anything. I just stared at her. I was backed up against the wall, the cold plaster poking through my thin shirt.

"Tell them," she repeated, her smile vanishing.

"Aunt Muriel, please."

"I want you to tell them I'm innocent, that it's all a misunderstanding."

She said this in a soft, pleading tone, as if she were asking me to clean up the breakfast dishes. And at that moment, even though her fingers were still digging into my skin, and I knew about all the things she had done, I found it hard to think of her as a criminal. I was in the position of either sending her to jail or saving her.

"She . . . she's my aunt," I said to the policemen.

They ignored me.

"Let her go," said a policeman, "or I'll have to take action."

"She's not armed," I said quickly.

They still ignored me.

Aunt Muriel looked me in the eye, and I felt my resolve, if I'd ever had any, starting to melt away. I'd thought that my knowledge might change things, that I'd be hardened to her. I'd thought I'd see images of Tom Wheat and Tyler flashing before my brain, and I'd want to see her punished. But in that moment, all I saw was the woman who was Zan's mother, the nice person who gave me Christmas presents, who took us to the zoo and the mall. I saw the woman who used to sing to me when I had trouble sleeping at her house. Aunt Muriel wasn't a criminal; she was my family.

Out of the corner of my eye I saw Lieutenant Dillard moving slowly across the room, working his way up behind Aunt Muriel. She had her back to him and didn't notice.

"You see, Abby and I were over here looking for intruders. We thought we heard someone in the basement. We were just about to look. Maybe you'd care to join us."

"Let go of the girl first," the policeman repeated.

"But she's my niece. Are you saying I'm not allowed to touch a member of my own family?"

Lieutenant Dillard was almost behind her now.

"Don't hurt her," I said meekly.

At that moment Lieutenant Dillard grabbed Aunt Muriel from behind, knocking her away from me. I spun into the wall, bumping my head. I heard her scream, a small desperate sound, like someone on a roller coaster as it starts its frightening descent.

"You just don't understand," she moaned. "Abby, tell them! Please!"

My bottom lip trembled. I felt tears welling up in my eyes.

"I think she killed Tyler," I mumbled through my tears.

Rod Stone took a step toward me, shaking his head in disbelief.

"And Tom Wheat," I said.

"Abigail, you're lying. She's a notorious liar," Aunt Muriel cried. "She's spoiled rotten, do you know that? A hotshot congressman's daughter. She's been totally protected. She has a completely distorted view of reality."

"Mrs. Ramsey," said Lieutenant Dillard, "you have the right to remain silent. Anything you say can and will be held against you in a court of law."

"Oh, stop."

"You have the right to an attorney. If you cannot afford an attorney——"

"I'm not poor! I've always had money!"

"——one will be appointed to you. Do you understand your rights as I have explained them?"

"Leave me alone," she said quietly.

"Take her out to the car, Sawyer," Lieutenant Dillard said to one of his men. Sawyer came toward Aunt Muriel with handcuffs.

"No," I said, without thinking. Then, as

they all looked at me, I said, "Do you have to do that?"

Lieutenant Dillard said, "It's not necessary. Just take her out to the car and call in to headquarters. I'll take a look around here."

As the policeman went out with Aunt Muriel, she threw a look over her shoulder toward me, and it wasn't a kind one.

"I'm sorry," I said softly.

Lieutenant Dillard put a hand on my shoulder after they had gone out.

"Are you all right?" he asked.

I nodded slowly, but I wasn't at all sure.

"You don't have to be sorry, you know."

I didn't answer him.

"Take a look around," Lieutenant Dillard said to the other policeman. "Start in the basement. And be careful."

I looked across the room and saw Rod Stone there, his face stalled in an expression of shock.

"Is it true about Tyler?" he half-whispered.

"I think so."

"Let's not jump to any conclusions," Lieutenant Dillard said.

"How did you find us?" I asked.

"I took your advice," the lieutenant answered. "I called Rod and he gave me a few interesting details. Particularly the cases of wine he and Tyler had found in the house. I knew about the robberies in Clark Ramsey's winery, and I began to ask myself, why does this wine business keep cropping up again and again? In my work, anything that repeats itself is usually important."

"It's not wine. It's drugs," I said.

Lieutenant Dillard nodded solemnly. "I suspected something along those lines."

"Sir? I think you'd better come down here and take a look."

My heart sank. Had they found Tyler's body?

Lieutenant Dillard headed down the stairs into the basement. Rod and I followed.

"Maybe you'd better stay," he warned us.

"No," Rod and I said in unison.

He could see it was pointless to argue with us.

We followed him down into a dark, damp room with the musty, unused smell of an empty cellar. It was almost completely dark, but I could tell the floors were cement and the walls bare cinder block.

"Where are you, Sergeant Hill?" Dillard called out.

"In here, sir, below the stairs."

We worked our way around behind the

stairs, following the distant beam of the flashlight. There was a door underneath, leading into a small opening. Lieutenant Dillard went in first, then Rod, then me.

A bare lightbulb hanging from the ceiling showed us the contents of the room.

Lying on a mattress, gagged, his hands and feet tied, his eyes open but vacant, was Tyler.

"Is he dead?" Rod asked. His voice was almost inaudible, but I could hear it shaking.

"No," said Lieutenant Dillard. "He's in shock."

They took the gag off first, then went to work on the ropes. Rod and I were standing together, and without knowing it I had gripped his arm and was squeezing it as hard as I could.

"Are you okay, Ty?" Rod asked quietly.

"Don't talk, son," Lieutenant Dillard said. "Just keep still."

Without knowing it, Rod and I had inched our way over to him. I could have touched him, but something stopped me.

"Please, move back," Lieutenant Dillard said. "Give him room to breathe."

The lieutenant took me by the shoulders and pulled me back. Tyler still had the same blank stare, as if he didn't possess a single thought.

"Tyler, come on, look at me," Rod said. "Do you remember us? Do you know who we are?"

Slowly Tyler looked in Rod's direction. His eyes blinked and gradually came to life.

"I know you," he said slowly.

Then he looked at me.

"But I've never seen her before in my life."

Chapter 26

≈≈ He kept insisting that I was a stranger, even as they loaded him into the ambulance. He said it loudly, harshly, getting angry every time I tried to move closer to him. Finally I gave up and didn't fight it. I rode in silence to the hospital with Lieutenant Dillard and Rod Stone. Once or twice Rod tried to offer some kind of consolation—"He's in shock, he doesn't know what he's saying"—but I kept remembering that cold, blank stare, and I was afraid it would be a long time before he remembered who I was. A long time, if ever.

Rod and Lieutenant Dillard spent a few minutes in the hospital room with Tyler. Although they were going to keep him overnight for observation, he was essentially okay. Malnourished, exhausted, disoriented, but nothing he couldn't overcome.

Lieutenant Dillard gave me that good news, and as I listened to it I stared at Rod's face, hoping for some sign of encouragement. He wasn't offering any. When Lieutenant Dillard went away to make a phone call, Rod sat down beside me and put a comforting hand on my arm.

"He'll come around," he said.

"So he still doesn't know me."

Rod shook his head.

"If it's any consolation, he knows me. He knows most of the details of his life. He just draws a blank when it comes to you."

"Why should that console me?"

"Because it means he'll recover. It'll come back to him. It just takes time."

I nodded slowly, trying to believe him.

"Believe me, Abby, I tried," Rod said. "I told him all about you. I told him what you looked like, where you lived at the lake, where you were from, that you were a congressman's daughter. Nothing seemed to work."

He paused, rubbing his thumb along his lip thoughtfully.

"What?" I asked.

"Well, I was just thinking. When I said 'congressman's daughter,' something seemed to register. It was like he . . . flinched. I don't know, it was weird. But I could tell it meant something to him."

"Of all the things to remember about me," I said quietly.

"It'll come back to him. I believe that."

"Well, he's okay. That's what's important. He really is okay."

Rod put an arm around me and gave me a quick hug.

"Thanks," he said.

"What for?"

"You saved his life."

I shrugged. Somehow it didn't seem that way.

"I should have listened to you before. I almost waited until it was too late. But you. You really cared about him from the very start. I know you love him. I told him that."

"I told him that, too," I said. "But he doesn't remember."

Rod and I said goodbye outside the hospital, making vague promises to keep in touch. Then Lieutenant Dillard drove me back to the house. During the drive, the events of the day seemed to topple down on me like a landslide. I closed my eyes, wanting to sleep. I kept hearing something going over and over in my head, like the chorus of a song.

Congressman's daughter. Congressman's daughter.

I wasn't sure what to make of it. But just as I drifted off, I remembered something else, something Lieutenant Dillard had told me.

Anything that repeats itself is usually important.

TYLER

Chapter 27

〓 I used to hate fall. I couldn't stand letting go of those long sunny days, the sticky-hot evenings, the smell of cut grass and suntan lotion, the sound of frogs and crickets talking me to sleep. Depression would take hold of me in September and wouldn't let go until the first nice day of spring. I was a summer junkie.

But that September, I welcomed the cool evenings and the brassy leaves, the snap of dried twigs and the crunch of grass. I enjoyed putting on shoes again, wearing a shirt every day, as if that helped me put distance between myself and the world. I no longer enjoyed feeling exposed.

"What doesn't kill you makes you stronger." I had heard people say that a thousand times. My father always dismissed that truism, like every other one he ever heard.

"Nonsense," he used to say. "What doesn't kill you probably should have."

But I disagreed. The incident at the lake had

nearly done me in, and as the days passed and fall approached, I did feel myself getting firmer, thick-skinned, and ready to face the world. Eager for it, like someone looking forward to a tennis match.

That's the difference between me and him. I came back. Dad couldn't. Dad didn't.

When I was tied up in the basement of The House, I had a lot of time to think. I was afraid the whole time, but after a while I just got used to the fear. Then I devoted a lot of that time to thinking about my father. Strangely enough, it was the perfect opportunity. No distractions, nothing to make me turn away. I just stared straight at the past.

I thought I was just mad at him for the way he died. He had been so perfect up till that moment, so wise and strong, and that final act was a betrayal of everything he stood for. I really believed my anger at him was because of that one, irrational moment. But the truth was, I wasn't just mad about the way he died. I was mad about the way he lived.

My father was a skeptic. He couldn't take anything for what it was. He had to dig beneath the surface, expose every lie, find the truth at any cost. I inherited a lot of that from him, and for a long time, I thought that was a great quality to have. But what I found out at the house across the cove is that when you start picking at holes, you better be prepared to get buried in them.

There is something else I know now: my mother isn't to blame for what happened to him. But I didn't discover that while I was locked in the basement. I found it out later, after I got out of the hospital and went back to Flanders. Back to my aunts' house, to see her.

For the first time ever, I figured my mother's state of mind was a small blessing. She'd never understand what had happened to me at the lake. She'd never have to read the newspaper articles. She was protected from all that had happened by the walls she had been so busy building.

I visited her every day for a couple of weeks. She didn't look too bad. Her face was lined and tired, but her eyes had some life left in them. She still dressed carefully (or my aunts dressed her), making sure everything matched. Her hair was combed, and she had on makeup. She even wore earrings. To look at her, you'd think she was just anybody's mother, living anybody's life.

Some days she acted like she didn't recognize me, even though I suspected she did. Those times were bad. She'd turn her back on me and stare at her lap, never speaking to me except to tell me to leave her alone.

But on some days she was perfectly clear-headed. She'd fidget nervously while I talked, and she'd laugh too loud from time to time, but she knew I was her son. She even told me to sit up straight once.

It was during one of those times that she told me something about my father she'd never told me before.

"You know what his problem was?" she asked me suddenly, without warning, while we were playing checkers.

I understood she meant Dad.

"No. What?"

She looked away from me and said, "He had no faith."

"In what?"

"Anything. Anybody. That's why he quit law school. That's why we never had anything, or went anywhere. He couldn't see the point. It made me so mad. He couldn't enjoy his life with me and you until he figured out the point."

I sat very still, fingering a checker piece, wondering if I should talk. She turned and stared straight at me, as if her concentration had never deserted her in her life.

"Well, for heaven's sake, you can't always

see the point of something. Just because you can't see it doesn't mean it's not there."

I smiled a slow smile.

"Am I right, Tyler?"

"Yes, Mom. You're right."

And she was.

Chapter 28

I moved in with Rod's family when they came back from their vacation. It may sound strange, but I was pretty content with my situation. Rod's folks were good to me. They treated me like a son. They cared about me, and Rod and I felt like brothers.

I still had my mother. She wasn't whole, and she probably never would be. But the good days were reassuring, and I knew that where there was one, there had to be more. I still had my father, too. Not perfect, the way he used to exist in my memory, but real. A guy who knew a lot about some things, and nothing at all about others.

Zan Ramsey's mother went away. The newspapers covered the story for a while, but eventually let it drop. There was never a trial. Instead, the lawyers made some kind of deal. Rich people have a way of getting out of trouble and disappearing when they want to. Zan and her father kept on living in town. Occasionally I glimpsed Clark Ramsey walking down the street in Flanders, looking a little bent and apologetic, but always sharp and clean, with a little bit of pride lingering around him.

Sometimes I felt tempted to say something to him, even shake his hand. I knew that in a strange way, he was less lucky than I. A lot less lucky, and a lot more alone.

One of the hardest things for me to come to grips with was Tom Wheat's death. I missed him, almost the way I missed my father in the early days. I couldn't believe there was just an empty space where all that thought and energy used to be. It was strange, but if he hadn't died, I probably wouldn't have missed him at all. I would have gone back to school and never given him a second thought. The thing that kept going over and over in my mind was how innocent he was. It made me think of my father's dog, Old Sport, and the way he had come to such an unsuspecting end. He had died trying to help. His loyalty had killed him.

I went back to school and got on with my life. I began to look into scholarships for college. There was a time when I thought I wouldn't bother, that maybe I would just go on building docks for the rest of my life. But ambition started to swoop down on me, and I thought I might go ahead and try to be an engineer or an architect. I wanted to build bigger and more lasting things.

I was making a lot of progress on the road to recovery, and everyday things were starting to concern me again. Like getting a haircut, buying spiral-bound notebooks for school, and jogging five miles a day. I was starting to believe I could put that strange summer behind me, just get rid of it like old clothes.

Then came that day in late September. It was a Friday and I was leaving school, heading out to the secondhand Mustang I had bought with some of my savings. Nothing fancy, just something to move me around and keep me from being a burden on the Stones. As I started out across the parking lot, I saw Zan Ramsey approaching me, moving fast, her dark hair swaying back and forth across her shoulders. She smiled directly at me, and I stopped walking until she reached me.

"Hi," she said. "Would you do me a favor?"

"I guess," I said, a little too stunned to think clearly. I had barely spoken to her since those days at the lake. We hadn't discussed anything, even when we first saw each other back at school.

"Walk with me," she said.

"Where?"

"To my car."

I walked. I couldn't see a reason not to.

I studied her face as we crunched across the gravel. She was still a beauty, but she looked different somehow. Her jaw didn't jut out the way it used to, waiting to take on the world. She seemed more cautious and unsure of herself. Suddenly, she was just a little bit human. And because of that, I liked her more than I used to.

"If you're feeling sorry for me, you might as well cut it out," she said.

"Why would I?"

"Let's see, my family's fallen apart, my reputation's in the toilet . . ."

"Nobody blames you. And you've got your dad."

"You're right! I suddenly feel like singing."

"Look, I'm not in a position to feel sorry for anyone."

"That's true. Maybe that's why I think we could be friends."

I shrugged, feeling a little nervous.

"I could always use a friend," I finally said.

She smiled and chewed on the end of a piece of dark hair.

"I could, too. Eric dumped me, you know.

I'm bad for his image. But if that's how shallow love is, I can do without it."

"You'll find someone else," I said.

"Maybe. Either way, I'll live."

We were approaching a shiny white BMW, which I had to assume belonged to her. Suddenly I saw someone leaning up against it. The sunlight was pouring down on her. She looked painted out of pastels, all blonds and blues and soft pinks. Her eyes landed on me and wouldn't move away.

Zan and I stopped, and Zan turned to me with a crooked smile.

"Do you remember my cousin?"

I said nothing.

"Well, she's here for the weekend, so you have plenty of time to get reacquainted."

I still couldn't speak. She moved away from the car, closer to me, and I let my eyes wander across the parking lot, to some trees in the distance.

"I've got a yearbook meeting," Zan said. "It'll only take half an hour, if you guys want to wait for me. If not, I understand."

Zan walked off then, her dark hair swishing and her tanned arms moving gracefully back and forth. I watched her, needing a place to look.

"I know you remember me," she finally said.

Though I still didn't answer, I allowed my eyes to meet hers. They were so pretty, prettier than the lake became in my imagination during the months that I was away from it.

"I always knew it. For a while I couldn't understand why you denied it. But I always understood you better than you thought. It didn't take long to come to me."

"I have to go," I said. My voice sounded croaky.

"No you don't. And even if you do, I'll follow you and make a scene. So you might as well stand here and listen to me."

I stood and listened.

"I guess I'm supposed to admire you. You were protecting me. You were thinking about my reputation. And maybe that's noble. But the thing you didn't get is that I'd rather have *you*."

I swallowed hard and made fists to keep my hands from shaking.

"Anyway, you didn't protect me from anything. You must have seen the papers. 'Congressman's Daughter Involved in Murder Scandal.' But then a better scandal came along and my father's little story disappeared. That's the great thing about Washington: there's always a bigger story somewhere."

I still didn't say anything. I didn't tell her

that I'd seen all the articles, read them over and over, cut them out and put them under my pillow. Not because of the stories themselves, but because of the pictures. Her picture.

"In a way it's my fault," she went on, "telling you how hard it was to be a politician's daughter. I was only trying to make you comfortable with me. I wanted you to know that I had problems, too. That's what I get for baring my soul."

She laughed lightly.

"And I guess those lectures from Uncle Clark didn't help, either. You believed all that. You thought you were obligated to stay away from me. You bought the whole package."

She stopped talking. For a long time we stood and listened to the sound of cars leaving the parking lot, gravel spinning, radios blaring—all the harsh and happy voices of people with no problems. It always seemed that way from a distance.

Finally I said, "Why shouldn't I have bought it?"

"Because, Tyler, that class-gentility stuff is dead. At least for me it is. The whole business at the lake should have taught you that. People with money are just the same as anyone else. Just as ready and willing to do desperate things. There's nothing separating us. Nothing real."

I let my eyes drift back in her direction. She was closer than I thought. I could have easily touched her.

"The thing is," she said, moving even closer to me, "I'm not sure I really understood all this stuff before I met you. I thought I knew that people were all the same, and that money doesn't really change that. I knew it here," she said, pointing to her head. "But not here."

She put a hand over her heart, and I felt a coldness inside me start to melt away.

"Abby," I said, in a whisper. It had been such a long time since I'd said her name out loud. Her smile told me she'd been waiting a long time to hear it.

"What?" she asked. "What is it, Tyler?"

I had learned this lesson before. To love someone meant to let go. It meant putting my well-being into someone else's hands, trusting that person to take care of it. My father had not taken care of it. This I knew. But I also knew that if I truly meant to forgive him, I needed to try again.

I kissed her. Or I let her kiss me. She put her arms around my neck, and I held on to her.

When the kiss was over I held her at the slightest distance and stared into her unforgettable eyes.

"I never stopped loving you," I said.

"I never stopped hoping," she said back.

I smiled at her. The lies and mysteries were out of the way now. All that was facing us was real life.

Abby

Chapter 29

My father gave up his seat in the House and we moved to Durham, North Carolina. Mom was from there originally and she wanted to be near her relatives. She'd always imagined this quiet life, Daddy hanging his shingle on Main Street and being a small-town lawyer, Mom staying at home canning vegetables from our backyard. I thought it was some kind of fairy tale. Nobody could really live like that, I said to myself. But we did.

It took me a while to adjust. I was used to activity—going to Tyson's Corner and George-town and riding on the Metro all over Washington. Suddenly I found myself riding my bike everywhere and hanging out at Dairy Queen and going to bake sales. It was weird at first, but then I started to like it. I could walk home after dark without fearing for my life. Within two days I knew everybody on my block, and within a week I knew everyone in my school.

In some ways, it reminded me of Flanders. The days were slow and lazy and comfortable. No one was in a hurry; no one had anywhere special to be. The only thing that was missing was the lake. And, of course, Tyler.

He wrote to me often. So did Zan. Her letters were still fat and flowery and smelled of perfume. His were short, with scrawled handwriting on notebook paper. When I'd write back to them I would try to sound witty and carefree, but eventually I'd break down and admit that I missed them both.

Guys at school were already starting to ask me out, and I said yes to one of them. His name was Dave and he was a nice guy. He took me to a movie and then for pizza, and he was funny and charming and said all the right things. But seconds after he'd kissed me good night, I couldn't remember much about him. I couldn't remember the jokes he'd made or the color of his eyes or what bands he liked. I remembered the first time I saw Tyler, how I felt like I'd been struck by lightning. He'd been with me from that moment on. His face, his voice, his smile. Everything about him was like a song that was stuck in my head. A beautiful song.

I invited Tyler to the homecoming dance. He drove down in his Mustang, and when he got out he handed me an armful of red roses. That night he wore a dark blue suit and a tie, and he looked like something out of a magazine. I could picture him years in the future, and I wondered if I'd know him then. I had a feeling that Tyler was just going to get better and better as all the bad times he'd had moved further and further into the past.

We slow-danced under the colored lights and the papier-mâché victory arch. Tyler put his lips against my ear and said, "You're the prettiest girl here."

I laughed. "Somebody better tell the homecoming queen."

He kissed me, in full view of everyone, including the uptight vice principal. Then he said, "I'll never forget you."

It was sad, the way he said it, as if he were telling me goodbye. But I knew what he meant: no matter what happened to us over the years, we'd always be connected. Because even though Tyler and I had spent most of our lives apart, that strange summer we grew up together.

After the dance, Tyler stayed in the guest house in the backyard. I sat in my room, holding the roses in my lap and staring at the light in the guest house, occasionally seeing his silhouette pass across the curtain. I thought about sneaking out there to be with him, but I decided not to. I just sat there thinking of him, knowing where he was, and that he was safe.

BEST OF THE BEST BOOKS FOR YOUNG ADULTS

> "*Titles commemorating a quarter century of quality writing and distinquished publishing for young adults.*"
> —ALA's Young Adult Library Services Association, 1994

CHILDREN OF THE RIVER, Linda Crew
0-440-21022-4
$3.99 / $4.99 Can.

ATHLETIC SHORTS, Chris Crutcher
0-440-21390-8
$3.99 / $4.99 Can.

STOTAN!, Chris Crutcher
0-440-20080-6
$3.99 / $4.99 Can.

SEX EDUCATION, Jenny Davis
0-440-20483-6
$3.99 / $4.99 Can.

VISION QUEST, Terry Davis
0-440-21026-7
$3.99 / $4.99 Can.

EVA, Peter Dickinson
0-440-20766-5
$3.99 / $4.99 Can.

KILLING MR. GRIFFIN, Lois Duncan
0-440-94515-1
$3.99 / $4.99 Can.

ONE-EYED CAT, Paula Fox
0-440-46641-5
$3.99 / $4.99 Can.

SIXTEEN—Short Stories
by Outstanding Writers for Young Adults,
ed. by Donald R. Gallo
0-440-97757-6
$4.99 / $6.50 Can.

THE FRIENDS, Rosa Guy
0-553-27326-4
$3.99 / $4.99

AMAZING GRACIE, A. E. Cannon
0-440-21570-6
$3.99 / $4.99 Can.

WE ALL FALL DOWN, Robert Cormier
0-440-21556-0
$3.99 / $4.99 Can.

THE OUTSIDERS, S. E. Hinton
0-440-96769-4
$4.50 / $5.99 Can.

DOWNRIVER, Will Hobbs
0-553-29717-1
$3.99 / $4.99 Can.

THE SILVER KISS, Annette Curtis Klause
0-440-21346-0
$3.99 / $4.99 Can.

THE SOLID GOLD KID, Norma Fox Mazer and Harry Mazer
0-553-27851-7
$3.99 / $4.99 Can.

ACE HITS THE BIG TIME, Barbara Beasley Murphy and Judie Wolkoff
0-440-90328-9
$3.99 / $4.99 Can.

ARE YOU IN THE HOUSE ALONE?, Richard Peck
0-440-90227-4
$3.99 / $4.99 Can.

THE YEAR WITHOUT MICHAEL, Susan Beth Pfeffer
0-553-27373-6
$3.99 / $4.99 Can.

DEATHWATCH, Robb White
0-440-91740-9
$3.99 / $4.99 Can.

THE PIGMAN, Paul Zindel
0-553-26321-8
$4.50 / $5.99 Can.